Holly-May Broadley-Darby has a passion for writing wherever she can. She is the author of *Zombie Killers*, and the sequel is in progress.

Youngest in her family, Holly-May was born in a small village called Hurstpierpoint in West Sussex, before moving at the age of nine years old to an island, the Isle of Wight, where her interest in writing began to flourish. In her spare time Holly-May likes to draw, write, read, surf and try new hobbies. She has a love for animals and enjoys walking her dog Lucy who is a Jack Russel cross Chihuahua.

For my family and friends who have always taught me to follow my dreams, you know who you are.

Holly-May Broadley-Darby

ZOMBIE KILLERS

AUSTIN MACAULEY PUBLISHERS™

LONDON • CAMBRIDGE • NEW YORK • SHARJAH

Copyright © Holly-May Broadley-Darby (2021)

The right of Holly-May Broadley-Darby to be identified as author of this work has been asserted by the author in accordance with section 77 and 78 of the Copyright, Designs and Patents Act 1988.

All rights reserved. No part of this publication may be reproduced, stored in a retrieval system, or transmitted in any form or by any means, electronic, mechanical, photocopying, recording, or otherwise, without the prior permission of the publishers.

Any person who commits any unauthorized act in relation to this publication may be liable to criminal prosecution and civil claims for damages.

This is a work of fiction. Names, characters, businesses, places, events, locales, and incidents are either the products of the author's imagination or used in a fictitious manner. Any resemblance to actual persons, living or dead, or actual events is purely coincidental.

A CIP catalogue record for this title is available from the British Library.

ISBN 9781786299994 (Paperback)
ISBN 9781787105065 (Hardback)
ISBN 9781787105201 (ePub e-book)

www.austinmacauley.com

First Published (2021)
Austin Macauley Publishers Ltd
25 Canada Square
Canary Wharf
London
E14 5LQ

Thank you to my mum, Sue, for helping me proofread, listen to me read it over and over and always being there for support.

Thank you to my dad, Keith, for believing in me and supporting me through the entire book.

Thank you to my big sister, Sophie-Rose, for always being there and loving me for being me.

Thank you to Aunty Caroline for always encouraging me.

Thank you to Mrs Christine Collier for always believing in me even when others didn't.

Thank you to Maya Sattar and Gemma Thompson for always being there by my side through thick and thin.

Thank you to everyone who has helped me to get where I am with their patience and encouragement.

Table of Contents

Chapter 1 — 11
Safe and Sound

Chapter 2 — 18
Old but Gold

Chapter 3 — 25
Scared to Be Lonely

Chapter 4 — 32
Bloodstream

Chapter 5 — 40
Know No Better

Chapter 6 — 47
Don't Promise Me

Chapter 7 — 55
Nothing Holding Me Back

Chapter 8 — 62
Courtesy Call

Chapter 9 — 70
We Should Have Known

Chapter 10 — 77
Burning Hell

Chapter 11 — 84
We Should Have Known Better

Chapter 12	**91**
The Betrayal	
Chapter 13	**98**
The Lab Plan	
Chapter 14	**105**
Room 179	
Chapter 15	**112**
Bite of Death	
Chapter 16	**119**
Take a Chance	
Chapter 17	**126**
The Injections	
Chapter 18	**133**
Never Safe	
Chapter 19	**140**
A Cure for a Bullet	
Chapter 20	**147**
Spirits of the Past	

Chapter 1
Safe and Sound

Mankind didn't know how it all began, but it did. They thought something like this would never happen but they were proven wrong.

It all began on a beautifully silent dark hilltop; a boarding school covered in ivy with heavy oak doors, securely shut, stood tall towering over the town below. A pale looking girl stared out of her dormitory window aimlessly overlooking the gravel car park, trying to block out the sound of the cleaning of the dormitories.

A small old fashioned boarding school stood behind theirs as it cowered in the shadows of the darkness that the Oak Forest Boarding School left behind it. Both boarding schools were surrounded by trees swaying violently for miles, reaching the town, as the caves nearby echoed from the heavy winds. A storm drew closer as thunder bellowed and lightning bolts flew out of the sky in the far distance.

It was an average Friday afternoon for the pupils at Oak Forest Boarding School but unfortunately it didn't stay that way for long. Zack and Daisy sat in class studying science, quiet as mice as they listened to the endless ticking of the clock. The sound filled the deafening silence as the clock counted down the minutes until 4pm.

Thirty minutes seemed like a lifetime as Daisy slumped over her desk, letting her short plaited brunette hair partially covering her worksheets. Her dark blue sparkly top hung loosely either side of her shoulders with an army coloured badge pinned onto it. She had black slim jeans tucked into her white and black trainers, showing the bright red shoelaces that were tied up perfectly. She let out a long exhausted sigh as she gently closed her eyes, letting her pale blue eyes disappear within.

"I just want to sleep or eat. Food sounds good," Daisy complained as she turned her head towards Zack who sat to the right of her.

Zack: a young boy with deep mahogany brown messy hair and emerald green eyes, reached into his blue and red striped rucksack. As the sun shone through the window onto him, flecks of gold strands of hair flickered. He pulled out a chocolate bar, handing it secretly over to Daisy underneath the table.

"You're the best friend ever," she replied breaking a piece off and popping it in her mouth.

"Yes... friend," he said to himself, "Nothing else, just a friend."

Leaning back on his chair, all the girls twirled their hair between their fingers as they stared at Zack adoringly. A sparkle glittered in their eyes while they watched his every move admiring him as they smiled, trying to flirt. They loved everything about him including his navy blue top with a black water proof jacket as well as his ripped brown trousers. Zack had nearly every girl in the school falling in love with him except the one girl he really loved.

The one girl he truly loved sat next to him seeing him as nothing more than a friend, so he thought. Every day was torture to him as he sat chatting to the girl he loved without her knowing his true feelings for her. Zack didn't want to tell her how he felt, so he didn't ruin their friendship. If being friends was the only way to talk to her then he would be nothing more than a friend.

Daisy was unique and Zack knew she had a rough time understanding the term of love. Mrs Peters, the science teacher suddenly stood up showing her tall narrow body. She slammed a book down, making everyone jump as every pair of eyes focused back on her. Her plain grey suit matched her personality as she began talking very slowly.

"15 minutes till the end of the class. I hope you've all done your homework!" Mrs Peters said loudly as her voice echoed of the walls.

"Yes, Mrs Peters," everyone answered together.

"Good. Now over the weekend, I don't want anyone in this room, especially if you're thinking about trying to create a 'cure'. I'm looking at you Ella. My brother is already failing at that and he's a scientist," Mrs Peters shouted.

The room filled with laughter as Ella turned bright red, feeling angry and embarrassed. Her dad was a scientist, maybe he wasn't the best at his job but she was proud of him nonetheless for trying to help save the world. Unfortunately, her aunt didn't understand his work when she worked with him.

She thought he was mad; mixing bottles of extremely toxic chemicals with other toxic liquids to create something new and strange. Sometimes he found a cure to a disease; other times he just made a disgusting colour that filled the room with deadly clouds or vile smells.

Mrs Peters left her brother and all of his scientific research after he accidently turned her fingernails to a dark shade of purple. When she tried to rub it off she found out that it was permanent. So she quit and became Ella's boarding school teacher instead.

The class was listening to their teacher when all of a sudden they heard an alarm, coming from the parking lot. A distraught, high pitched scream silenced the class and froze the teacher to the board. The two seventeen year olds; Daisy and Zack scampered out of their seats as they barged past Mrs Peter's, who happened to have come in the room at the wrong time.

As they peered through the peep hole in the main door they saw Amy, a mysterious teenager whom hadn't spoken a word to anybody since her parents died when she was 5 years old, was trapped inside a vehicle as she had left early for a doctor's appointment and just arrived back wearing a complete black outfit showing off her bright red and black hair that dangled down her back. The only light thing about her was her dazzling pink lipstick that made her lips stand out against the rest of her.

"Help!" Amy screamed, yanking at the door handle in fear of her life.

Why isn't anybody coming? Where is everyone? Amy thought to herself. All of a sudden; a bunch of students came running over and started banging upon the windows violently. However, they weren't ordinary pupils – they were seemingly mutated.

Amy was stunned, her hazel coloured eyes widened. What had happened to them? Amy started to panic as she soon realised that they weren't pupils from her Boarding School, but from their rival Boarding School. What made it worse was that they weren't human anymore, they were dead!

"I… I want out! Help! They're going to kill me! Somebody… Anybody… Help me. Please!" Just then Amy screamed in horror as a zombie smashed its arm through the car window, now strongly grasped her left arm, piercing her skin with its nails.

Amy reached for her laptop, which was in her black handbag beside her. She smacked the zombie creature, hitting it hard on its head, hoping it would release her arm from its deadly grip. Unfortunately, its grip tightened more causing her arm to become painfully red as her blood flow slowed down. To make matters worse the creature started thrashing its head against the window, hoping to get in.

Zack and Daisy stood in the main hallway chatting as they tried to think of how to help their friend. They knew they had to think fast otherwise they would lose their friend.

"I'm a bit scared, to be completely honest," Zack explained, "I'm afraid of thunderstorms and I can see one coming."

"Everyone has fears but she needs our help!" Daisy replied as she ran quickly to the door, "So put your fears aside and help me to help save her."

"Fine, count me in but don't laugh if you hear a high pitched scream," Zack grumbled.

A short slim boy with blonde neat hair ran towards them. He was wearing a blue jumper with a clean white shirt underneath neatly tucked into his grey baggy trousers. His top button on his shirt was missing, showing the shape of his collar bone below.

"Wait," Lewis yelled as he ran towards them nearly tripping over.

"No, we can't wait. She needs help, she's our friend," Daisy continued stubbornly.

"That's why I want to help," Lewis argued.

"Are you serious?" Daisy froze to the spot in shock.

"Yes. Don't sound too surprised," Lewis laughed; even though he knew it wasn't a joking matter.

A young girl with short brown almost black hair tied up high in two ponytails skipped towards them wearing a green baggy top with a red broken heart imaged in the middle of her top with the words ripped apart in black underneath and blue skinny jeans.

"You can count me in too," Ella shouted.

The four of them rushed out of the room as they heard Students screaming around them. Zack and Lewis knew that the only way for them to get Amy out of the car and to safety was to distract all the zombies which surrounded the car that Amy was in.

"Come on Lewis. Stay close and follow me," Zack commanded.

"Don't tell me what to do," Lewis said with anger.

Lewis hated being bossed about by people, all his life he had been a nerd who was bossed about by the cool kids. Since last week he had finally had enough of it and had stood up for himself. His life had changed a lot over that week; when he walked down the hallways he didn't get called names or tripped over, instead people kindly greeted him.

"Just follow my lead, for Amy's sake," Zack said, not giving a second thought of what he had just said.

As Zack and Lewis dashed out the doors, Ella and Daisy swiftly and silently shut the doors behind them. Making sure any zombies nearby couldn't get into the building as they didn't know much about these zombie like creatures.

"Climb, climb as high as you can," Zack whispered, pushing Lewis behind the nearest tree. Lewis, for once, did as he was told because he knew it was a life and death situation, not just for Amy but for him and Zack too. He climbed; pulling himself up with his weak delicate hands as he moved his feet one by one onto the next branch.

Suddenly a branch snapped beneath one of his feet making one of his shoes slip off, falling to the ground. A loud thud sounded across the parking lot as three zombies turned and started walking slowly towards them. Zack looked up as Lewis gained his strength, still pulling himself up the tree.

"Keep climbing. Quick, they're coming," Zack whispered hastily.

Zack couldn't wait any longer the zombies were closing in on them. He quickly jumped behind a nearby bush where he could still see Lewis very clearly but Lewis couldn't see him. Lewis looked around, searching for Zack as he started to panic.

"Where are you Zack? Don't leave me!" he screamed attracting the attention of the zombie's.

"I'm only down here Lewis. Now stop screaming, you're attracting the attention of the zombies," Zack said as he looked over at Amy.

The zombies were leaving her alone because Lewis had screamed. Now Lewis was quiet; the zombie's attention was facing Amy again, putting her in danger. Zack had a plan to save her but he needed Lewis for it and he didn't know whether he would agree to it.

"Climb higher and scream as loud as you can. You're distracting the zombies so I can help Amy. Then I'll be back for you," Zack explained as he slithered his way past the zombies.

"WHAT!" Lewis screamed in shock, "You're putting me in danger to save her!"

Zack ignored his remark once again as he continued walking over to the car. Zombies turned their heads and sniffed the air, they could smell Zack's blood beating through his body but they couldn't see him as he hadn't made a noise. He quickly ducked beside the car; keeping out of the zombie's sight, Zack tapped the window carefully once to get Amy's attention, making sure not to attract any zombies

"Finally, you took your time!" Amy whispered in delight.

"Follow me," Zack said, opening the driver's door.

Amy scooted her body across to the driver's seat, taking every movement with care. Zack grabbed her as he began lifting her carefully out of the car. A piece of broken glass cut into her leg, just above her black leather boots as she let out a painful scream. Zack's hand shot over her mouth to stop the screaming as he didn't want the zombies to come after them. A tear ran down her face from the pain.

"Don't worry; Daisy and Ella will help you once we get you inside," Zack explained, picking her up into his masculine arms, knowing she wouldn't be able to walk as one wrong move and the glass could go in so deep her leg would start bleeding badly.

"Okay," she whispered through the pain.

Blood floated through the smoke filled air as the car window smashed, letting splinters of shattered glass fall to the crumbling ground. Light pierced its way through the dying oak trees that towered over the broken down walls of the boarding school, letting glimpses of light show the zombies that surrounded the boarding school grounds.

Chapter 2
Old but Gold

The strong smell of Amy's blood covering the glass attracted all the zombies nearby. They turned and stared at Zack and Amy who stopped dead in their tracks. Each zombie started to moan as they began to walk slowly towards them; gaining more and more speed, the closer they got.

"Not again," Amy whispered as she turned her head towards Zack, facing away from the zombies.

"This is good, it gives Lewis the chance to escape and get inside but we have to out run the zombies as well, especially as I have to carry you because you can't walk with your leg like that. Okay?" Zack explained.

"Okay. I know," she replied.

Lewis began calmly climbing back down the dying tree as leaves gracefully fell around him. Gradually his feet touched the ground once again but as they did, a zombie looking pigeon swooped down with its dark grey wings widely spread through the air. Its red eyes glared at him as it began flying after him; he grabbed a stick and threw it at the zombie pigeon; trying to slow it down, giving him more time to run away from the dead creatures that roamed their school grounds.

Time was running out as the zombies paced after Lewis. Zack and Amy had already reached the safety of the building, but Lewis had fallen behind; they anxiously paused in the doorway with Ella, who had been awaiting their arrival. The group watched helplessly as the zombies gained on Lewis. They were defenceless as they stood waiting for him.

Ella huffed and began tapping her foot with anticipation. Would it be right for them to close the doors on him, leaving him for dead and saving themselves, circled through Ella's mind. No she couldn't do that, not to him. As much as the temptation clawed at her, she fought against the urges, she had to wait. She could not forget the compassion in which made her a human and separated her from the monsters outside.

"I'll take Amy to the medical room, to get her leg checked out," Daisy explained as she looked down at Amy's leg which was covered in splinters of glass and blood. The large piece of broken glass was still in her leg and Daisy knew if she did anything it would start bleeding even more, draining her body of its blood.

"Okay, just please hurry back," Zack said worriedly to Daisy as he turned his head back towards the door.

Amy wrapped her left arm around Daisy's shoulder as two older students ran towards them to help. One of them grabbed her other arm wrapping it round their shoulder as the other one cleared a path for the four of them to get to the medical room. Daisy looked behind her before they disappeared through a door leaving Zack and Ella to help Lewis.

"Lewis you can make it, just a little further," Zack shouted at him, "Come on! Run like your life depends on it because it does!"

"He's not going to make it," Ella said doubting him as she leant against the wall next to the door, "I can't watch but I can't look away! Hurry!"

"He will. He has to," Zack whispered under his breath, watching his friend run for his life.

"Come on!" Ella began screaming.

The two friends began shouting at Lewis with fear creeping throughout their bodies. They had to ignore their fear and encourage him to gain more speed in order for him to live and make it inside without any bite marks or injuries. None of them knew what the creatures could do or how strong they were but they did know one thing and that was that they meant business. These things weren't something to mess around with.

Everyone thought that zombie films weren't based on real life situation and that they were just something to scare people or question the future of humanity, those people were wrong because now they had to deal with being in a zombie apocalypse but they didn't know that this was only the beginning, the 1st phase of the apocalypse. This wasn't a game; this was real life, their lives!

As Lewis dashed inside a zombie quickly grabbed his leg through the small gap of the open door. They stared at the zombie in shock, the look of hunger rushing through its monstrous bloodshot eyes with dark purple like bruises surrounding it. Drool fell from its rotting mouth as a horrible stench escaped. Lewis tried to kick it away with his other leg, desperately trying to make it let go.

It was a terrifying sight as they saw part of the zombie's skin ripped and hanging loosely from its face; Zack pushed against the door as he saw more zombies come running towards them whilst it's grey bony hand was still attached to Lewis's leg. For a split second the zombie looked at Lewis as if he was confused but that second soon ended when Daisy came running towards her friends.

"I'm back," Daisy explained, before shouting, "Oh my god Lewis."

"Help me," Lewis screamed.

Ella grabbed her school pen from her bag and jammed it into the zombie's hand which was gripping Lewis tightly. Daisy suddenly grabbed Lewis's arms and began pulling him away from the zombie's grasp. The zombie let out a terrifying screech as it quickly let go, making Daisy fall backwards, hitting her head on the floor. Daisy quickly scrambled to her feet, ignoring the pain that pulsed through her head.

Rushing over to Lewis, who was shaking in his shoes, she took his hand and began helping him up. Ella and Zack leant against the door trying to shut it as Daisy moved Lewis away. Weights of hundreds of zombie bodies pushed against the door and with only two people trying to shut it; Ella and Zack found they were no match alone for the zombie invasion as their feet started sliding. Two of them alone didn't have enough strength to shut it.

"Don't just stand there," Zack shouted as he leant against the door.

"Help us," Ella screamed as she carried on pushing against the door, her feet were slowly giving up below her. She felt her legs turn to jelly.

Lewis swiftly rushed to the door, helping to push it shut yet the door still wouldn't stay closed as more zombies approached, not giving in. A few minutes later; Amy, who was limping on crutches with her leg bandaged up, came back with a bunch of students and teachers, all pushing tables and chairs.

"Here to help," Amy smirked.

"Finally... We needed help," Lewis replied as his foot began slipping under the pressure from where the zombie had grabbed his leg, ripping a layer of his skin with its grey infected nails.

He fell to the floor, pain flooding down his leg. Daisy grabbed his arm to help him up once again as she leant him up against the wall, out of the way. Students and teachers rushed to the door with stacks of chairs and tables. Zack grabbed Ella's arm as they both darted out of the way.

Daisy, Lewis, Amy, Zack and Ella watched as their fellow pupils barricaded the door, protecting their school and everyone in it. Many of the students had grown up treating the school as if it was their second home. All of the teachers acted friendly and kind towards everyone, making the school feel homely to them all. They weren't giving up, not as long as the school stood with no zombies inside.

Finally; they had finished, the door was secure. No one could get out and no one could get through; they were all safe within the walls of their school. Zombies could no longer get through the door. Suddenly, a loud shatter bellowed through the boarding school freezing everyone to the spot. That's when they all knew that no one was safe any longer.

A bunch of growls grew closer; as everyone turned around, there stood a zombie twitching and growling. It wore bloody ripped clothes which showed parts of its red raw skin; it had a massive bite mark in its left arm which had blood dripping down on to the floor, leaving a bloody trail behind it.

"Just great," Amy complained as she saw more zombies enter through the smashed window, "Now what?"

"We need to go now," Zack said, seeing the scared look on his friends faces, "we're not safe here anymore!"

"Okay," Daisy nodded as she replied, "Zack and I will help Amy and we'll meet you two outside."

"Is that okay with you two?" Zack asked, turning his head towards Ella and Lewis.

"Yeah, I guess. Not like we have a choice. Do we?" Ella responded sarcastically.

"Come on then Ella, let's go," Lewis said as he rolled his eyes, unhappy with Ella's sarcastic comment.

Lewis had never liked Ella, mostly because she was always being sarcastic or joking about everything. You could never have a serious conversation with her. Ella didn't like Lewis either as she found him to be too smart for his own good. He was always trying to prove himself to someone, always trying to be the smartest in the class. They both knew they had to put their differences aside in this new world.

Lewis and Ella ran to the first door but as they were about to enter the room, a bunch of zombies smashed through the glass windows. The zombies growled, their bodies twitched and clicked as they glared at the two of them. Lewis paused in his tracks with Ella hidden behind him as the dead slowly walked towards them.

"Maybe this way isn't the best way to go," Ella whispered.

"You got that right. Quick let's go," Lewis replied.

"You don't have to tell me twice," Ella answered as they both darted off in a different direction.

Zack walked in front of Amy; who was currently struggling with the pain and adjusting to the crutches. Her long black and red hair swung behind her as she limped in front of Daisy who kept her distance carrying Amy's bag as well as her own bag.

More zombies fled into the school as more windows smashed. The building which was a once nice Victorian style with fire places burning giving a cosy warm feeling was now overrun with deadly zombies that wanted every living thing dead. Luckily Zack knew all the ways in and out of the building as he always used to sneak out after curfew into town.

"Which way now?" Daisy asked, looking left to right and then behind her for safety.

"Left," Zack answered, "We're going through the backdoor in the kitchen. Don't worry; I know where the spare key is."

"How do you know?" Amy asked, looking up at Zack as the three of them paused.

"Let's just say, that's one of my techniques to sneak out without being caught," Zack said.

Amy's leg suddenly gave in as she collapsed to the floor in agony. Zack had no choice but to carry her till they were safe outside while Daisy carried her crutches and their bags. It seemed outside would be much safer than being inside a zombie infested school.

As they reached the kitchen; Lewis and Ella arrived a few minutes after them. They stopped and stared at their three friends as Ella turned around, seeing a large shadow move swiftly around the corner. They all heard very quiet growls.

"Hurry up. They're coming!" Ella whispered.

"Can you hold Amy please?" Zack asked as he turned to Lewis.

"Yes sure," Lewis answered as he smiled at Amy.

Lewis reached his arms out to take Amy from Zack, who quickly got searching for the key underneath a plant pot on his right. Amy blushed as she looked up at Lewis. For the first time since her parents had passed she felt happy to be near people.

Suddenly; Amy gave a slight moan of pain, as more blood leaked out of her wound. Zack reached his hand into the plant pot; covering himself in dirt, he squirmed around inside the pot as he picked up a key shaped object. He pulled the key out and quickly put the key in the key hole. He twisted it but as he did a few zombies came running around the corner.

"Quick, get in!" Zack shouted as he pushed his friends through the door. As soon as they were all in he slammed the door shut and locked it. While Ella and Daisy pushed a desk against the door.

Lewis and Amy let out a loud scream as they stared at a body lying on the floor in a pool of blood. It was covered in bite marks, scratches and splinters of glass. Muddy footprints led to the door and stopped at the body. Daisy and Ella tiptoed over to Lewis and Amy as Zack joined them. The five of them shook in fear as they looked at each other.

Flies had started to gather around the body as they dived into her flesh leaving little circles in her skin. All of a sudden a swarm of flies darted towards them, dripping with blood and saliva. The flies were now carrying the disease and had become part of the problem.

"Quick, the back door now," Daisy shouted as she pointed at the back door.

Amy was still in Lewis's arms and in a lot of pain as all of her friends ran to the back door. As they ran, they swatted the flies with the back of the hands, not thinking of their delicate skin. Daisy grabbed a cloth and began hitting the virus away, giving her friends and herself more time to run to the back door.

Zack rushed to the door, darting past the body and the killer flies. As he reached the door; the body began to move, clicking its bones as it stood up. He twisted the door handle before opening the door and escaping. One by one, his friends came running out as he slammed the door shut on the zombie face, trapping it inside.

Chapter 3
Scared to Be Lonely

Standing outside; they could feel the cold air rush over their skin, they could hear faint growls from behind them. Even though there were no zombies where they stood, they knew they were still not safe. Zack helped Lewis to carry Amy while they all ran together; knowing Lewis had an injured leg as well as Amy.

None of them paid attention to their surroundings as they galloped down a countryside lane. They could smell the rotting flesh coming from all directions, getting closer to them. The road got thinner and thinner the more they ran, almost until it was non-existent.

After an hour of running, they finally gave in as they collapsed from exhaustion on a bench at a bus stop. The pain in Amy's leg was starting to ease but she still couldn't walk properly without pain returning, let alone run. The group of friends started to relax, nearly falling asleep as they saw a herd of zombies approaching, running down the hill towards them.

The pack of zombies ran a lot faster than the ones they had dealt with at the school. Some of them fell over as they tumbled down the hill, showing no pain or memory of the person they once were.

"ZOMBIES!" Amy shouted as she hugged Lewis tightly for safety.

In the distance behind the zombies they could make out a faint outline of a car, speeding past the deadly zombies that were dripping blood with every step they took as they gazed at the moving vehicle in astonishment. A scream was heard from the car as the zombies started running towards it. As the car got closer to Daisy and her friends, it came to a stop as the girl in the car leaned across, opening the passenger door.

"Get in," the girl shouted.

They all quickly got into the car as the zombies got even closer. The girl who was driving began talking to everyone, in order to get a conversation going, so the atmosphere was more relaxed.

"My name is Scarlett. What yours?" Scarlett asked.

Scarlett wore a long dark purple sleeved top with a light purple vest over the top of it. She had a black choker around her neck which was covered in bloody handprints. Her long hair was the most amazing feature about her as they all gazed in amazement. It had loads of different shades of blue, starting dark at the top and going lighter the closer it got to the bottom.

Big ocean blue eyes stared at them as Scarlett waited for an answer. Ella wasn't sure whether they should trust the girl or not but at the time they didn't have much of a choice. It was either trust a complete stranger or become food for the dead.

"I'm Daisy; that's Zack, Ella, Lewis and Amy," Daisy explained.

"Is Amy alright, back there?" Scarlett asked.

"We could ask the same about you!" Ella replied before Amy could, as she looked at Scarlett's blood covered neck.
Lewis looked at Ella angrily; watching the corners of her mouth twitch irritably. Scarlett rolled her eyes, unfazed by Ella. Even though Scarlett didn't have to help them, she did, yet Ella was finding a way to get on the bad side of her. Amy raised her eyebrows, nudging Ella, unimpressed by her attitude.
"You think I didn't have to kill a few of those things to get here?" Scarlett answered, "I didn't want to but I would be dead if I didn't."

"Back to your original question... No, I'm not alright, my leg is hurting again but I'll survive," Amy said as she put her injured leg up onto Lewis's lap, "Hopefully."

"We're here to help you survive, Amy," Scarlett replied, nodding at her, "Your friends got you this far, I doubt there'll give up on you now!"

Amy smiled at Scarlett as she filled her soul with hope once again. She had never heard anyone say anything like that to her, not even her friends. Of course she knew her friends loved her and would never leave her as they had shown it over and over again but they had never said it to her face.

"You got that right Scarlett. We never leave one of our friends behind!" Daisy explained.

Scarlett could see the goodness within them all, even a little bit in Ella who she could tell didn't like her and she didn't know why but she couldn't care either. She wasn't there to make friends; she was there to survive the apocalypse, making friends was a bonus.

"Why don't we get to know each other a little bit," Ella said, glaring at Scarlett.

"That's a great idea," Scarlett said, trying to be nice to Ella.

"Do you have any family?" Lewis asked.

"I have an 18-year-old sister and a 19-year-old brother. My dad is in his late 30s and he's a scientist but also owns a farm," Ella answered before anyone else could talk.

(Ella liked her life how it was before hell took over earth. She never got along with her mum; they would always argue and fight. Her mum left when she was young and didn't stay in contact but it never bothered her. Ella worked on a farm her entire life with her family. She loved every day on the farm, waking up to nature.)

"I've got a brother who will be 19 in a few days. That's it; that's my family, my parents died," Amy said as she began relaxing.

(Amy missed her parents a lot of the time but being three years old when her parents had died, the memories had started to fade away. She didn't like the fact that the only memory she would have of them would be in photographs. Amy lived alone with her brother, who was her only living family member she had left.)

"I live with my dad. I have a younger sister called Joy who is 15 years old who lives with my mum. I don't see either of them at all now but oh well," Zack explained, trying to hide his feelings.

(Zack always wanted to see his mum but his dad would never allow it, he saw his sister in secret but his dad wanted nothing to do with their side of the family. His sister was only young and had never saw their father and nor did she want to. Their parents were the reason they couldn't be a real family and had to hide so many secrets.)

"I have a 21-year-old brother called Josh who is away fighting in the army. I live with my foster carer called Jane who I've lived with for years," Daisy said.

(Daisy and her brother had always been very close. Josh got Daisy a place to call home. It was Josh who got Daisy accepted into the Boarding School. He would do anything to protect his little sister and she would do anything to protect him. She missed her brother regularly, but he always wrote her letters so that she wouldn't worry about him too much when he was away fighting.)

"I have three siblings, all younger; Josie who is 9, Jay who is 12 and Nathan who is 15. I live with parents," Scarlett said as she thought of her sister alone.

(Scarlett's parents never cared about her or her sister as her parents only wanted boys. Since the day Josie was born, Scarlett had protected her. Josie and Scarlett always shared a bedroom, where the boys got a bedroom each. If either of the girls put a foot out of line, they would both be grounded but her brothers could get away with anything.)

"I live with both my parents but I'm the only child," Lewis said.

(Lewis always hoped to have siblings and always wondered why he had to be an only child. When he asked his parents they would always say they were too busy for him, let alone another child. He never understood why they even had him as they were always too busy to pay him any attention.)

By the time they arrived in town it had started to get dark as they looked closer they noticed; burning buildings, cars over turned, shop and house windows smashed. The sight was horrifying as the smell of death surrounded them. Bodies lay on the ground covered in bite marks with blood oozing out of them. Luckily there were no zombies left alive, only bodies with bullets piercing through their skulls.

Scarlett pulled the car over in a parking space as everyone grabbed their bags, getting ready to jump out of the car. They needed to collect supplies as the only things they had was the items they left the school with as well as what Scarlett had within the car.

"We will divide into four groups," Daisy explained, "Ella and Lewis go find food and drink. Amy you're staying in the car. Zack go find some medical equipment whilst Scarlett and I search the town for any survivors."

"Meet you back here in no more than two hours. There are 4 walkie-talkies in the boot of my car with 4 guns," Scarlett explained as she ran to the boot of her car and opened it.

"Everyone take a walkie-talkie and a gun," Zack said, "Amy keep your head down, the windows up and doors locked. Here's a walkie-talkie."

"Will do," Amy answered.

"Why do you have guns in your boot Scarlett?" Ella asked Scarlett, not trusting her.

"One, we're trapped in a zombie apocalypse and two, stop questioning me and get on with it!" Scarlett replied angrily.

Daisy and Zack stood awkwardly next to each other while they listened to Scarlett and Ella arguing. Silently the two of them walked to the boot, leaving Amy alone in the car.

"Both of you, stop and empty your bags in the boot. We need to make more room," Daisy commanded.

One person from each group grabbed a walkie-talkie and loaded their guns. Zack was first and instantly darted off, down the road to the right. Ella and Lewis both disappeared together in the opposite direction as Daisy and Scarlett ran off, vanishing round a corner and darting off down an alley.

Twenty minutes floated by as Amy sat in the car, fiddling with her fingers in boredom. Meanwhile Zack's luck had finally changed as he found four boxes full of medical equipment in a chemist. As he reached forward to open one of the boxes; Zack felt something cold pressed against his head. He turned around to see a teenage boy about 18 years old holding a gun to his head.

The boy had a dark grey face mask covering his mouth and nose. He wore black ripped jeans with a sleeveless black top. He had light brown hair that was hidden under his white and blue dotted hat. A piece of paper poked out of his trouser pocket as Zack stared at it curiously.

The boy pushed the piece of paper safely back into his pocket, out of sight before putting his focus back on to Zack. He seemed to be hiding something but Zack wasn't sure what.

"What's your name?" the boy shouted.

"Please calm down. I'm not here to hurt you," Zack said in a soothing tone, putting his hands in the air showing the boy that he wasn't a threat.

"I said… What's your name?" the boy repeated again, taking a step back as he clutched the gun tighter.

"I'm Zack. Now please put the gun down and tell me your name."

"Cameron… My name is Cameron. What do you want? Why are you here?"

"My friend hurt her leg; I was just coming to get supplies to help her. Please Cameron put the gun down! I mean no harm, she's in a lot of pain and I need to get back to her."

"Fine but you have to help me first."

"With what?" Zack asked a little bit confused

"My little sister disappeared, I can't find her. I'm extremely worried about her. She was behind me one minute and then gone the next. I need to find her," he replied anxiously.

Forty minutes went by as Ella and Lewis rushed in and out of empty shops searching for food and water. At last they ran into a fully stocked supermarket. Each shelf contained different varieties of food and drinks as Ella rushed to the sweet isle, grabbing a chocolate bar.

She ripped the wrapper off before taking a massive bite out of the chocolate bar; she licked her lips happily as Lewis stared at her in shock. Somehow she had managed to get chocolate all over her face.

"You're an animal!" Lewis explained as he folded his arms.

"Sorry, I'm a girl and we love chocolate, well I do at least. Also it's the apocalypse; soon this stuff will be gone. Who do you think will be alive to make chocolate?" Ella replied.

"Let's get the food and drinks that we need and get back to our friends!"

"Fine!"

They unzipped their bags, stuffing loads of items into their slightly torn school bags. Ella grabbed all the nice looking tin food with expensive looking labels on them, whilst Lewis grabbed all the bottled water he could find, not caring what the labels looked like, and putting it into his bag, making sure both bags were completely full before leaving.

Even though they knew it wouldn't last them very long, they were proud to contribute to the team. They both liked feeling that they mattered and that they were doing something to help. Lewis kept guard as Ella seized hold of her walkie-talkie and said, "LE to A, we have the food and water. We're on our way back."

Chapter 4
Bloodstream

Scarlett suddenly heard Ella's voice over the walkie-talkie as she removed it from her pocket, listening to what Ella had to say. Meanwhile, Daisy was opening a glass door which led to an indoor shopping centre as the two of them entered.

"What does LE and A mean?" Scarlett asked Ella over the walkie-talkie.

"Ella, Lewis and Amy, obviously," Ella replied, "What did you think it meant?"

"No idea, I don't talk in code!" Scarlett said sarcastically.

"Shut up you two," Daisy interrupted as she grabbed hold of the walkie-talkie from Scarlett and tucked it in her own pocket.

Scarlett and Daisy walked through the shopping centre in utter silence with the only noise coming from their shoes, tapping against the floor. Daisy remembered shopping here with her brother, back when it used to be full of happy customers carrying bags as they dashed into the next shop.

Now the shopping centre was abandoned and every store within was broken and destroyed. Loads of plastic bags drifted through the main walkway, with litter spreading widely across the bloody floor. Unused clothes with tags still attached laid crumpled on the floor, as they stepped carefully over it.

Silence was soon broken when they heard a scream. They quickly rushed around the corner, following the sounds of the screams, to see a timid girl about 14 being cornered by three zombies. They could see the terror in her blue watery eyes, dripping down onto a graze on her cheek which was sore and irritated. Her long brown hair tied up into a ponytail was tangled with leaves attached. She was wearing dungarees with a pink long sleeved top.

Before Scarlett knew it she had grabbed hold of the gun, pulling the trigger. The bullet flew straight through the zombie's heads, making the zombies collapse on the floor. One of the zombie's heads snapped off, rolling across the floor leaving a bloody trail as the little girl squealed. Daisy and Scarlett rushed over to her.

"What's your name?" Daisy asked.

"Lindsey, ma'am," Lindsey politely whispered.

"I'm Daisy and this is Scarlett," Daisy said.

"Have you been bitten?" Scarlett asked.

"No, ma'am," Lindsey said, shivering from the spiteful cold.

"Let's get some spare clothes, then head back to Amy and the others," Daisy explained.

Daisy and Scarlett slowly began to walk away, hoping Lindsey would have started walking behind them but as the two of them turned around, they realised Lindsey had not moved an inch. She was standing still, not making any sudden movements as Daisy calmly walked towards her.

"Are you coming?" Scarlett asked Lindsey.

"I can't!" Lindsey replied.

"Why?" Daisy asked.

"I have seemed to have lost my brother. Have you seen him?" Lindsey said with a worried look on her face, "We got split up when those things arrived."

"I'm afraid not," Daisy said as she took a quick glance at Scarlett, "sorry."

"How about we go and get the clothes, ask the rest of our group, if they've met anyone who's looking for their sister?" Scarlett explained.

They continued walking, entering the first clothes shop they found, splitting up to cover more ground. It didn't take them long to pick some items that were suitable for their unique styles and the apocalypse, as well as for their friends.

When they had finished choosing the clothes, they quickly jogged over to the changing rooms to get dressed.

After they all got changed, they decided to meet up with the rest of their friends as it had already been an hour. As they arrived back at the car, Zack stood to the left of Cameron while Ella and Lewis stood to his right.

"Lindsey," Cameron shouted as he ran towards her, "I've been so worried."

As soon as Lindsey's eyes locked onto her brothers, she began running towards him. Tears streaming down her face as she wrapped her arms tightly around him. Meanwhile, Daisy and Scarlett showed their friends the bags of clothing they got. They threw the bags, one by one, into the boot of the car before slamming it shut. Zack turned around to see a flock of zombies scampering towards them.

"GET IN THE CAR!" Zack shouted.

At this point they were all shaking with fear as they all saw more than one hundred zombies rushing towards them. They jumped into the car as quickly as they could, with their breathing getting faster. Zack turned the car key to get the engine to start, slamming his foot down on the accelerator as they sped off. He drove straight through the zombie horde, watching each rotting body hit the car, skidding of the bonnet in front of them.

Lindsey began crying, as the night sky spread across the empty void above them. She shuddered with terror as Cameron and Scarlett attempted to calm her down, telling her to take deep breaths as they did the same to hide their own fear. They looked out of the windows just as a zombie came out of nowhere, making a sudden dash for the car causing Scarlett to jump. The zombie dropped to the ground as she heard the back tyres crushing what was left of the decaying body, spreading its guts across the road.

The car engine began making spluttering noises, eventually grinding to a sudden halt, stopping dead in its tracks as they noticed a symbol of a petrol pump warning light on the dashboard, they had run out of fuel. They all jumped out of the car, grabbing hold of their bags. Zack grabbed Amy, holding her in his arms as he knew she couldn't outrun the zombies.

Without a second thought they all started running, leaving the car doors wide open. None of them looking back but they could tell that the zombies were close behind. They couldn't out run them forever; they needed somewhere to hide allowing the zombies time to leave.

All of a sudden Ella's foot got caught in a crack in the road, making her trip, spraining her ankle. A burning sensation shot up her ankle as she screamed in agony. Amy looked over Zack's shoulder but the zombies had already surrounded her. It was too late, they had all started munching through her stomach, into her guts.

Blood splattered everywhere as Ella let out one last painful ear-piercing shriek. Amy glanced back for one last time as she looked back to see Ella standing up, regaining her balance. Her limbs began to click with her head falling forwards. Ella's bloodshot eyes glared into Amy's before snarling showing her rotten teeth that were stained yellow as she darted towards them with a limp. She joined the crowd as she limped after her old friends; she had lost all of her humanity along with her memories.

Unexpectedly a group of six young looking people jumped into the road with loaded guns and weapons securely in their hands. Four of them had already begun shooting at the zombies behind Daisy and her friends who were ducking their heads as they ran towards them for safety.

"Quick, run!" A young boy shouted.

The boy who had shouted was now staring at Daisy letting his long curly brown hair blow in the wind. He turned to a young lad with dark skin, who wore a red long sleeved top with cardboard strapped onto his arms as well as his legs, covering his blue jeans for protection. Half of his brown hair was shaved off while the other side had a lot of layers.

"Zoe, go help that boy and his friend," the leader commanded.

The leader turned to a girl with short dark brown and purple striped hair. She had tanned skin with a skull tattoo covered in red and yellow flowers, dancing around the skull, at the top of her arm which was partly covered by her blue short sleeved top. Zoe had dark brown eyes that were partly covered by her side fringe.

"Sir, yes, sir," Zoe said before running towards Zack to help him carry Amy.

"Follow Jason back to the hideout," the leader shouted.

They followed Jason; a guy with black curly hair, wearing a black and green jumpsuit. Jason was taller than all of his friends as Daisy looked like an ant compared to him. His entire face was covered in freckles and cuts with sunglasses covering his eyes, they all began running back to the hide out.

In the distance they could still hear the gun shots as the zombies screamed, dropping down dead! Daisy and her friends couldn't turn back to help the new group as they would be putting Amy and themselves in too much danger. They had already lost Ella; they didn't want to lose Amy too. A few minutes later the leader and his other three friends came running towards them.

"RUN!" one of them shouted, "We've run out of bullets."

A zombie was very close as one of the girls fell, hitting her head on the ground. Her gun escaped from her grasp as she pulled it from her pocket, slipping out of her reach. She didn't have time to get it so Scarlett grabbed her own gun and pulled the trigger, shooting the zombie in the head. The bullet penetrated its skull passing through its brain and out the other side as yet another one dropped down dead. She grabbed the girl by the arm, lifting her onto her feet.

"Now run, don't fall again!" Scarlett told the girl.

The girl didn't even look behind her but she knew she had to run in order to live. It didn't take them long till they had reached the hideout which was two doors covered in ivy and leaves. The leader quickly put in a five-digit password 14709. Click! The doors opened and they all ran inside.

Zoe slammed the doors shut. Once closed the leader quickly grabbed hold of some metal chains, wrapping it around the door handles before securing it with padlocks. They stood in utter darkness for a few minutes before Zoe ran her hand against the wall to find the light before switching them on. The light showed the dampness and ivy which was creeping up the walls.

"Welcome to our safe zone. I'm Adam, the leader here. That's Lucy our commander and James is the organiser," Adam explained, "Zoe is the first aid trainer, she has basic knowledge in medical history."

They were thankful for the help that they were given however they didn't understand how the new people could call this place a safe zone. Adam was definitely in charge and was respected by his group. Daisy hoped that someday her group would be like theirs, with no arguments or disagreements.

"And my job includes checking for bites! I also fight the zombies," Zoe said giving some sass whilst interrupting Adam.

"Rebecca helps with the fighting, training and cooking," Adam continued as he pointed to a blonde haired girl before turning to a tall lad, "Jason is the deputy commander."

As Adam said that Jason winked at Amy, who instantly blushed as she snuggled into Zack trying to hide her reddened face. She yawned, as her eyes slowly began to shut, she tried her hardest to keep them open but she couldn't stay awake. Amy gave in as she fell asleep.

"I'm Daisy, that's Zack, Scarlett, Amy, Lewis, Cameron and Lindsey," Daisy explained showing that she was the leader of her group, "Unfortunately Ella died whilst getting here."

"Okay, first question; what happened to your friend in your arms? She's not bitten, is she?" Adam asked looking over at Zack and Amy.

"She's not been bitten. There's a shard of glass in her leg. It got stuck there when we were trying to escape from our boarding school at the start of the outbreak," Zack said.

"Zack, can you and Amy please follow Zoe," Adam said with concern, "Zoe is the best one here with some medical knowledge. She will be able to help your friend and check her over."

Zack quickly followed Zoe out of the room and down the long hall to the medical room while Daisy, Scarlett, Lewis, Cameron and Lindsey all stayed with Adam and the rest of his group. Daisy wasn't fond of the splitting up idea as Amy was quite vulnerable due to her being injured but Daisy seemed not to have a choice in the matter.

"Should I check them for bite marks? Jason can take them to the hall afterwards so that they can get something to eat and drink as they must be hungry by now," Lucy asked

"I don't mind showing them to their rooms afterwards," James said quietly.

"Yes, to the both of you," Adam laughed.

"Come on then, don't have all day," Lucy said.

They started walking towards a room which had a huge sign saying "WARNING, BITE ROOM! ONLY PEOPLE WHO HAVE BEEN OR ARE BEING CHECKED FOR BITES ARE ALLOWED." It sent a giant shiver down their spines as they carried on dawdling down the cold, eerie narrow corridor. On each side there where rooms with at least three padlocks on, a few of the doors had bloody handprints dragged across the cracked windows.

"What are these rooms used for?" Daisy asked even though she knew that she wouldn't like the answer.

"The first corridor isn't used anymore except for junk; the second corridor is where I will take you into separate rooms so that I can check you all for bites. The finale corridor is off limits to everyone except Adam and the doctors as that's where we keep the zombies. The doctors are dissecting and experimenting on the zombies to try and find a cure," Lucy answered.

"Who are they?" a 19-year-old lady asked.

The lady wore a doctor's uniform with black leggings and a black top which showed part of her clothing underneath the uniform. She had long black hair that was tied up into a ponytail, leaving none of her hair loose and completely out of her face. Her green ember eyes stood out because of this.

"This is Daisy, Scarlett, Lewis, Cameron and Lindsey, they're here for their check-ups," Lucy explained, "This is Brianna, one of our doctors."

Chapter 5
Know No Better

A male doctor who appeared to be around the same age as Brianna walked towards them. He wore a dark blue top with a bloody apron covering his white trousers. The man wiped his sweaty blood covered hands cautiously on his trousers. The male doctor had brown eyes that suited the colour of his wavy hair which stood up uncontrollably in all directions.

He gave some paperwork over to Brianna, covering the important and confidential information with a blank piece of paper. As he began walking away Doctor Brianna shouted his name, making him stop dead in his tracks. He showed instant fear in his face, turning pale as his name left Doctor Brianna's mouth

"Yes miss?" he answered as he gulped, showing the terror within his eyes.

"Doctor Collins, please can you take the two boys; Lewis, and Cameron and check them for any bite marks?" Doctor Brianna asked, "I'd recommend that you take their blood pressure at the same time!"

Her eyes were fixed upon him as she spoke. A piece of bread fell out of his pockets, falling onto the cold hard floor. He bent down to pick it up, his hands trembling as she trudged towards him. Looking up at her; he saw one of her eyebrows raise unimpressed.

Before he came to the safe zone; he lived with his mum in a flat. Each time his mum would go to work at the hospital, she would make her son a strawberry jam sandwich. After the loss of his mum, it left him with nothing to remember her by apart from precious old memories of growing up. He thought of her every time he looked or ate a piece of bread.

"Stealing food again Collins, I see," Brianna said.

He stared at her as he felt the bread crumble within his hands, a tear seeped through his eyes and down his face. One of the rules of the safe zone was no one was allowed to steal food or take more than their food portion for the day. He had broken that rule.

"I won't tell this time, if you do as I've asked," she continued.

"Of course Doctor. Boys, please follow me," Doctor Collins replied.

As the boys disappeared, Lindsey gave a worried look to her brother as she watched him leave once again. The last time they were apart she was nearly eaten by zombies. Even though she felt safe with Daisy and Scarlett's company, she felt lost without her brother's presence to protect her.

When they had finished being checked, they were shown to the main hall by Jason. Amy and Zack had finished their check up and came rushing out to join Scarlett, Lewis, Lindsey, Cameron and Daisy. Amy had been given a pair of crutches as well as a wheelchair just in case.

Jason chatted away happily to Amy, enjoying her company as they all walked to the main hall. Lindsey skipped happily beside her brother. Entering the dark hall, they could smell the strong dampness and mold and see vines that crawled up the rigid walls. Lights were flickering as they swung loosely from the ceiling which was covered in cobwebs and half eaten flies. Groups of people stopped eating and stared at them as they stood in the middle of the hall.

Another group slowly entered the hall, all dressed in dark clothes; they were as quiet as mice, slowly but swiftly walking over to a table in a darkened corner with the only non-working light in the entire hall, they all sat down. The corner wasn't only dark; but it was also cold, as chills sent shivers down their backs! Some of them wore scarves and hats whilst others didn't seem to be phased by it.

Zombies could be heard from where Daisy and her group were standing. Even though they couldn't see them it still frightened many of them especially young Lindsey. A young lad walked over to Scarlett and took her hand as he tried hard to flirt with her.

He wore a tight black vest top with a pair of sunglasses dangling from it. His dark blue trousers were covered in wet sloppy mud, hiding all the rips. What Scarlett hated about him the most, was the fact that his light brown hair looked as if a toddler had cut it with safety scissors without him knowing.

"You're absolutely gorgeous. There's no way you could be single," the boy said, flicking his hair out of his face, allowing his green eyes to show.

"He flirts with every girl he sees. Don't be fooled," one of the younger girls, wearing dark clothing, warned her.

"Go away, you jerk," Scarlett said to the boy, stepping back, "Go waste somebody else's time!"

"How rude of me, I didn't even tell you my name. I'm Damion. Yes, the Damion and you are?" Damion asked, ignoring Scarlett's nasty words.

"None of your business, now leave me alone," Scarlett frowned, pushing him away

"Or what, my precious little angel," Damion said trying to push his luck as he moved closer.

"Or you will see what your precious little angel is really made of! Now leave me alone you annoying little weasel," Scarlett said as she turned her back and walked away.

The girl that had warned Scarlett about Damion had also been watching their entire conversation as she wanted to know what was happening. This way she would see if Scarlett was a girl to be messed with or not. She could already see that Scarlett did not like Damion and had learnt a lot by watching her attitude towards him.

"That's rich coming from you," Damion said as he burst into a wicked laughter.

All of a sudden; Scarlett's face turned red with fury as Damion blew the last straw. She might have had to take it once from her family but she didn't have to stand it from him.

He meant nothing to her, and didn't feel any guilt of what she was about to do.

Without hesitation, her leg began swinging, kicking him straight in the balls as he fell to the ground whimpering in pain. Scarlett looked down upon him, raising her eyebrows as she turned sharply and walked away. Proudly joining her friends, they all patted her on her back.

"That's how you teach boys like him," Cameron smirked.

"Did you really have to do that? You could have just shouted at him instead of resorting to violence!" Lewis mumbled.

Cameron and Daisy looked at him unimpressed as the words left Lewis's mouth. He gulped as he felt his friend's eyes glued to him. Even though Lindsey understood where Lewis was coming from, she also agreed with Scarlett as he had not backed away when he was asked too.

"I agree but sometimes you have to teach them a lesson, especially if they continue to bully you," Lindsey said as she rubbed her foot on the back of her ankle.

"High five Scarlett," Daisy said, ignoring Lewis and Lindsey's remarks.

The young mysterious girl who had been watching them, walked over to where Scarlett and her friends stood. The girl had gorgeous dark red hair which flowed down to her waist, she was wearing a black long sleeve top and light blue ripped denim jeans with a pair of long black boots up to her knees. A detailed drawn on rose could be seen on her wrist, she pulled her sleeve down to cover it, as if it was supposed to be a secret.

"Well done. You taught him a lesson. I'm Emily," she said, "When I first arrived he kissed my hand. My brother beat him up for it as I'm only 14. Adam and a few of his friends, broke the fight up and took my brother to a room to calm him down. Luckily Damion hasn't tried anything since."

One of the main rules of the safe zone was absolutely no fighting allowed under any circumstances and will not be tolerated. Even though Emily's brother only did what he felt like he had to do in order to protect his little sister. Even though he still broke a rule, Adam wanted everyone to know that violence wasn't tolerated. They needed to keep the peace between the human race and make sure everyone was at least civil with each other.

"That's awful; I'm glad your brother helped you! I can't stand Damion," Scarlett answered, "I can't stand any one like that."

"Why don't you come and sit with my group," Emily said as an older boy rushed over to them.

"I'm sorry about my sister," he said grabbing her by the wrist, "She always wonders off."

"This is my brother Jake. The one I told you about. He's 17," Emily said giving Scarlett a wink.

Jake had dark brown spikey hair that lays flat covering his forehead, hiding his beautifully golden brown eyes. He wore a dark blue top with black stripes on the cuffs of his sleeves. There were no rips in his trousers; instead parts of his legs were covered in plastic that was sellotaped tightly around his knees and ankles.

His smile gradually made Scarlett's stomach fill with butterflies as she gently fiddled with her sleeves awkwardly looking away. She noticed he also had a rose drawn on his wrist which she figured meant something to the two of them, joining them together in some way. Scarlett's eyes instantly lit up as she started speaking, moving her hair out of her face to flirt a little.

"I'm Scarlett," she shyly introduced herself.

"What an unusual but pretty name," Jake said, smiling at her.

Scarlett laughed, she felt her knees buckled with the weight of her body tumbling down upon her as her cheeks turned a gorgeous ruby red colour. Emily was a nice kid who happened to have a really hot older brother. Scarlett couldn't help herself as she followed them over to their group. It was love at first sight for the both of them.

Daisy, Zack, Amy, Lewis, Lindsey and Cameron waited with Jason who was busy explaining everything about the different types of groups within the safe zone. Some of the groups wore dark clothing while others wore bright colours that could attract even the smallest of creatures, not to mention the zombies whose eyesight had gotten better.

Lucy had left them standing in the middle of the main hall with Jason, while she left to join her own group which was called the techs. They were mostly called that because they had a fascination with modern technology as well as past-tech and could easily fix anything.

"Everyone in here is the proud future of the human race and the existence. There might be more survivors out there and it's our job to help find them, so we can bring them here," Jason explained.

"Where can we sit," Amy asked as she looked at Jason, "most of the tables look full."

"Table number 7 is free. Just go and get your food from Justine," Jason pointed at an old lady wearing a hair net, "All you have to do is state your name and age. Then Justine will give you some food."

With that Jason slowly turned around, carefully kissing Amy softly on the cheek as he started walking away giving Amy one last glance before walking out of the doors. They slammed shut behind him as he left. Before Amy could say anything, he ran back in as he walked over to Daisy.

"I nearly forgot to say; in half an hour James and Mia will come to escort you to your rooms. Also Daisy, Adam has demanded your presence in his office before you leave to go to your room," he said before rushing off again.

"Well let's go and get some food," Cameron explained.

"I hope they have bacon," Lewis replied.

"I'm so hungry, that I could literally eat a horse! I don't care what they give me as long as it's edible," Amy explained.

Scarlett joined her friends as the eight of them rushed over to Justine who was serving food to a young man. As he turned around, Scarlett noticed it was Damion, a shocked look quickly made its way on to his face. He started trembling as his brown eyes began watering. Damion quickly moved out of the queue, letting Scarlett and her friends skip in front of him.

"S… S… Scarlett!" he stuttered.

"What do you want Damion Weasel?" Scarlett asked with a fierce tone.

"Please… Please don't h… h… hurt me. P… P… Please," he begged.

"On one condition," Scarlett said as a grin sneaked onto her face.

"W… W… What, I'll d… d… do anything. A… A… Anything you ask! Just please don't kick me again," Damion Weasel carried on stuttering as he panicked.

"STOP FLIRTING WITH EVERY GIRL!" Scarlett shouted angrily, flicking her hair with sass.

Some people even cheered while others loudly laughed. Most of them were happy that someone had finally put Damion in his place. He had flirted with too many girls and broken too many hearts while he had been there. Only a few people had the courage to stand up to him but no one had ever done it like this or had him trembling in his shoes.

"Deal," Damion said as he hung his head in shame before walking off, dragging his feet.

While Scarlett was busy chatting with Damion, Daisy and the rest of their group had got their food, sitting down at their table. They noticed it was covered in huge amounts of dust as they placed their plates down.

"Well let's eat," Cameron said as he gave a little quiet chuckle before rolling a piece of ham and shoving it into his mouth.

"I'm starving," Lindsey said quietly as she took a petite bite of her cheese sandwich.

Chapter 6
Don't Promise Me

Scarlett was very proud of herself. She grabbed hold of her food and swiftly joined her friends at their table. As she sat down Daisy quietly told Scarlett about the commander wanting to meet her, however she didn't know the reason why. All their friends tried to listen as they ate their long desired food.

"That's weird. I wonder why they didn't say anything else?" Scarlett briefly said, placing her cutlery on her plate as she turned to face Daisy.

"No, not a clue," Daisy replied, taking a big spoonful of cheesy mash potato carefully trying not to make any mess while eating it.

As dinner time came to an end, two middle height ladies and three tall men all wearing army uniforms rapidly walked over to where Daisy was sat with her friends. They stood silently at attention behind them, letting them finish their food and conversation before interrupting.

"Which one of you is Daisy Territory?" one of the ladies asked, as she stepped forwards towards the table.

"I... I... I am," Daisy answered nervously as she began stuttering.

"Please come with us," one of the males said with a firm voice as he pointed at the door, "Let's go!"

"Am I in trouble," Daisy asked in a worried tone

"We're not allowed to give you any information, it is highly classified," an older man, who was also in army uniform, answered.

Daisy shyly stood up, and the army soldiers escorted her out of the main hall, leaving her friends behind at the table as they stared at her with curiosity. Daisy and the mysterious army soldiers instantly vanished as the doors swung shut behind them.

"Please, just tell me if I'm in trouble. I've never done anything bad in my life, I swear. Please just tell me. What have I done?" Daisy said in a panicky voice.

"We can't tell you anything Daisy, we've already told you that!" one of the men said, raising his voice at her.

As they arrived at Adam's office, one of the female soldiers wrapped a blindfold around Daisy's eyes, throwing her into complete darkness which caused her to worry and panic even more. They waited outside his office as seconds ticked by, turning into minutes. All of a sudden Adam shouted enter giving them permission to step a foot into his office.

The lady, who had unexpectedly blindfolded Daisy, carefully pulling her by the arm and directed her into the freezing cold office room. A sharp shiver crawled down her spine as the door creaked loudly, slamming shut behind them. Without warning the lady stopped, letting go as she took a few steps back and stood at ease.

Her blindfold was slowly removed. There in front of Daisy stood her older brother Josh who was taller than an average 21-year-old. His dark blue eyes held a variety of stories within, his messy brown hair was hidden underneath his battered old army hat. This made sure all of his hair was out of his face, allowing everyone to see the scratches which covered his face.

He wore a green camouflaged top and black baggy trousers, that had a gun holster holding a fully loaded gun in it. As she looked closer, she noticed he had a bruised neck which made it look like he had been strangled as well as splashes of dried blood around the bruises.

"Josh!" Daisy screamed, overwhelmed with joy.

Daisy was completely shocked to see her brother standing there as she was under the impression that he was elsewhere fighting in a war that protected him and his country. Josh slowly walked towards his sister who he had not seen in a very long time, as he took his hat off revealing his hair which flopped down across his face. He picked her up as they both burst into tears of happiness.

"You have no idea of how much I've missed you, it's been way too long," Josh said slightly sobbing as he held her tight, "I promised you that I would be back soon!"

"I've missed you lots too, it's not been the same," Daisy answered as she began to cry with pure happiness, "How did you even get here and why? I thought you were away fighting for your country!"

"I have been fighting in a horrific war however it's not the type of war that you'd think of... We had been fighting against the zombies but we unfortunately lost. I came back due to being overrun with them, too many of them and not enough of us. I heard on the news about your boarding school, and after hearing that I just knew that I had to come home to make sure my precious baby sister was safe. I kindly asked my army friends to fly me over as soon as we could, I had to make sure that you were alive. You're my priority. I also wanted to say happy birthday."

"With or without this zombie apocalypse; this is still the best 18th birthday present that you could ever get me, even if you're a week early," Daisy laughed.

"You know that I'm always thinking of you, you're my family after all!"

"Don't worry Daisy, Josh and his friends are not leaving. They're staying with us to help protect everyone in this Village. Anyway it's getting late; James and Mia are waiting outside, to show you all to the rooms where you will be staying."

As Daisy and her brother opened the door, they were met instantly by James and Mia who were leaning against the walls impatiently, bored out of their minds and didn't enjoy waiting. Soon as they saw Daisy and Josh they began walking, then bolting not even waiting for them to catch up. Adam ensured everyone was out of his office as he locked it up, running towards all of the doors to make sure they were secure and zombie proof.

Daisy quickly ran up to Adam and kindly whispered, "Thank you, for everything," before she tried to catch up with her brother Josh.

It didn't take them long to arrive at their rooms as Daisy and all her friends had been placed in the same hallway which she was extremely happy about. They dragged their feet down a dull looking hallway that had four plain doors on each side. All the doors were painted pure white, making them look new and stood out against the dark dusty walls.

Daisy looked over at her brother before carefully opening the door to her new bedroom and entering. It was nothing like how her bedroom was at her old home. There was not a single drawing on any of the walls, like she had at home which she had done with her best friends. At home the other three walls were painted a beautiful blue colour but here they were painted in a boring, magnolia colour.

It was a middle sized square room with two single metal beds made up with new sheets on each bed in opposite corners of the room. A small chest of drawers stood beside each bed with a set of clean clothes as well as two reading books. Under each bed there was a long plastic box filled with lots of items to decorate the bedroom. A familiar face stared back at her from one of the beds as she looked around the room.

"Hey roommate," Scarlett said with a grin on her face.

"You're my roommate," Daisy answered happily as well as in shock, "At least it's someone I know."

Daisy shut the door quietly before quickly running over to the bed and falling onto it with exhaustion, it didn't take her long to fall asleep. The next morning: everyone woke up at 7am to a really sharp high pitch alarm shrieking painfully through everyone's ears.

As Daisy sat up, she rushed to the door before yanking it open and running to her brother's room. She wanted to make sure that it wasn't a dream. Her heart pounded harder and harder as she reached his door. She knocked softly, with the sound of the alarm becoming overbearing as no one came. She knocked again but still nothing, not a sound came from inside the bedroom, no movement at all.

"Josh?" Daisy said. worriedly.

She launched herself down the corridor, thoughtlessly knocking everyone out the way. Instinctively she headed to the hall. A thundering bang echoed through the building as she threw herself at the doors, opening them at such a speed she fell onto the cold floor with a thud. Grabbing her sore arm, she looked up and noticed the room was full with hungry people. Her cheeks turned crimson, freezing with embarrassment whilst everybody gawked. Keen to help, her brother got up from his seat, striding towards her.

"You okay? Did the zombies get in?" Josh asked

"No. You weren't in your room?" Daisy replied, breathing quickly.

"You thought it was a dream, didn't you?" Josh asked.

"Exactly," Daisy said, giving him a big hug.

Josh knew exactly how she felt especially whilst he was away as he would dream about home, his sister, celebrating birthdays, opening presents on Christmas day as well as searching for Easter eggs. He held his memories close to his heart. The only thing he didn't enjoy was waking up, knowing his sister wasn't beside him.

"Well I do have something to tell you. You've got a test," Josh explained, forgetting about his thoughts.

"Test, what test?" Daisy asked, "I'm not good under pressure!"

"I'm not allowed to say sorry sis but I've been told to have you there in two minutes. You'll be fine, trust me."

"Hopefully. I guess we'd better get going then."

The two of them rushed out of the room as Josh put his arm around Daisy's shoulder, walking beside her. Thankfully he had already done his test before breakfast, so he knew the way. After scampering down a lot of twisting corridors, like an ever-lasting maze, they finally arrived at their destination.

"I'll sit outside here," Josh said as he went to sit on the floor outside the room.

Taking a long deep breath, she entered into a dark room as she felt fear and worry take over her entire body. Daisy could feel her hands shaking as the door slowly shut behind her. Even though Josh had already taken his test, he didn't have his results. Everyone had to wait till tonight to find out.

Lights lit up once the door was fully closed. The test had officially begun. Dozens of holograms appeared; zombies, her friends, weapons, Josh, her parents and sadly even Ella. Seeing her felt like a new horrible wound that was infected; she missed her a lot, but she got along better with everyone else.

There was a gun, throwing knives and a bat lying on a metal table. A computer in the corner with photos showing a range of different style of clothes. Some clothes were black, camouflaged and also there was a few bright and colourful ones. Daisy instantly knew what to pick as she began clicking on the photos.

She clicked the photo of a black long sleeve top which had the words **Run-Shoot-Kill** on it, blue jeans, black boots and cardboard wrapped around her arms. Suddenly the clothes she picked appeared on her body, she was shocked but very impressed by their technology.

Next she seized hold of a gun before the holograms turned around to face her. She walked to the middle of the room in her new outfit and stood on the X, holding the gun down by her side. As soon as all of the holograms had turned to face her, an announcement bellowed through the speakers.

"In order to survive in this new world, you need to run, shoot and kill, even if you once knew the person. If they are a zombie, you need to kill them. It's that simple," as the announcement finished, the holograms started moving.

She let out a horrific scream as the holographic zombies faced her before a few began running whilst others limped towards her. Some of them left a bloody trail as well as guts behind them. Daisy tightened her grip on the gun with her hands and started shooting every zombie in their heads. She watched their lifeless old bodies crumple to the floor.

A soft growl could be heard behind her as she turned around, she saw her friend Ella as a zombie. Daisy dropped her gun in shock, as her dead school friend walked towards her, twitching her head uncontrollably as her jaw locked together. Within a few minutes Ella was coming face to face with Daisy as she fell to the floor, trying to seize hold of her gun.

"I'm sorry Ella," she whispered as a bullet hurtled through her head.

More holographic zombies arrived as she shot them all, letting the second to last bullet soar through the air and through the zombie's head. As the bullet landed on the ground, the hologram room stopped. The lights flickered continuously on and off.

"Now try and kill three, maybe four zombies… with only one bullet," the announcement said.

Three zombies appeared, standing next to each other and then another and another. To get them all with one bullet, she had to wait till they were perfectly lined up or it wouldn't work. She didn't know what would happen if she missed but she did know that she would have failed the test. Suddenly another announcement bellowed.

"We seem to be having a few technical problems, it's over loaded. It's all out of control. Try and survive, good luck."

Daisy threw herself behind a large bin, trying to hide as she waited for the zombies to line up. Minutes disappeared as Daisy suddenly yawned, drawing attention to herself as the zombies turned their heads and walked towards her. She backed away slowly. Finally; the zombies were lined up perfectly. Jumping out, she raised her gun, pulling the trigger as the bullet sliced through the air. Zombie's heads exploded drenching the walls with blood and rotten flesh.

The Hologram room had come to an end as Daisy had hoped she would never have to do it ever again. Seeing her friend like that, made her think of how much the world and her life had changed, but now they had to share the planet with zombies, who could evolve and adapt to their surroundings making them more or less dangerous.

An hour later: Daisy came out with a massive smile spreading widely across her face as she felt like she had done a good job and was extremely proud of herself. Daisy had successfully killed all the zombie holograms including Ella her friend which was tough but she managed to do it.

Chapter 7
Nothing Holding Me Back

Normally when someone dies, you're told that they're in a better place but Daisy knew that Ella and every dead person in the world wasn't. Nor were the living who had to fight now in order to survive. The human race was now living in a world that had turned upside down. Nowhere was safe as every turn you took could lead you into danger as you'd face more zombies.

"Daisy... Are you okay?" Josh asked, standing up "You've not said a word since you came out."

"I'm Fine!" She muttered, with no expression.

They strolled back to their bedrooms in utter silence unsure of what to say next as they waited for their test results. Josh left Daisy outside her bedroom as he entered his own room. She twisted the door handle, opening it and entering before slamming it shut behind her.

She dragged herself to a bed, feeling her anxiety creeping through her mind as she sat down and picked up a book. Luckily it was one of her favourites. Daisy laid down and opened the book, trying to block out the feelings of hopelessness within her. Whenever she was reading, she would often find herself lost within the pages, imagining herself as one of the characters and not trapped in the horrific world she now lived in.

Hours passed as Daisy carried on lying on her bed reading the second book of Harry Potter. The feelings that were once overwhelming her thoughts had now gone as she got distracted with every turn of a page. What she liked best about this book was the character's friendship. It didn't matter how tough life got, nothing could split them up.

A loud knock suddenly transported Daisy back into reality. She sat up, dropping her book with a fright. She wasn't sure whether the knock was real or just her imagination playing tricks with her mind, she decided to ignore it as she picked her book up from the floor.

A second knock on the door made Daisy instantly slam the book down on her bed and shoving it under her pillow. She flew off the bed and swiftly moved towards the door. As she pushed down on the handle, only letting it creak open a little bit a short man stood in front of her as she stared.

"I'm guessing you're Daisy Territory," the man said as he huffed impatiently.

"Yes, that's me," Daisy answered, looking puzzled.

"Here's your test results from this morning," the man explained, handing her a brown envelope.

Daisy closed the door, shutting the man up before he could get another word in. Once alone, she ripped the seal off the envelope and took the results out. She was frightened and a nervous wreck, as she held it in her hands. The results held her destiny at the safe zone, telling her what her job would be; a warrior, supplier, tech genius etc. Without thinking she started reading it out loud as her brother entered.

"Dear Daisy Territory, we are happy to inform you of the results for your test. You are now a fighter along with Zoe, Jason, Lucy, James, Jade, Cameron, Emily, Tyler and Zack. Training is every day at 2pm and 7pm. You will go searching for survivors at 10am. Meet everyone at the front doors at 9:30am sharp where you'll be equipped with everything you need. Yours sincerely, Adam."

Daisy wasn't sure how to feel, excited or worried, about it. She was looking forward to finding new survivors but she was scared about leaving the safety of the compound and going outside where the zombies were, especially after what had happened to her school and Ella.

"Are you okay sis?" Josh asked as she froze in place.

"I'm fine," Daisy replied as she sat down, leaning against the metal bars of her bedframe.

"I'll leave you alone, I guess," Josh said with pain in his eyes as he slowly walked out of her bedroom.

Once Josh had left, Daisy instantly scanned the names on the letter hoping that she had imagined seeing Zack's name. Daisy didn't want him to know but she had a massive crush on him since the first day she had met him. Instead of telling him; she hid her feelings not wanting to get hurt.

Her finger wandered across the list of names, passing everyone's until she found his. Unsure of how to feel or react, she flung her door open and ran to Zack's room. Without another thought, her fists were smashing against his door as the sound echoed through the empty hallway. Suddenly it opened and Zack was standing in front of her with the unopened letter in his left hand.

"You okay?" He asked awkwardly.

"Just open the letter already," Daisy demanded, taking a deep breath in.

"Why?" Zack questioned her, "Is something wrong?"

"You'll understand once you have read it," Daisy replied.

Zack looked at her, looking confused as he opened the envelope containing his results. He took the letter out and began to quietly read it. With his eyes locking onto the paper, noticing Daisy's name. He worriedly looked up, her eyes saddened as his arms dropped, letting the note fall swiftly to the ground.

"Is this true?" he asked.

"Yes," Daisy replied, staring at the floor in despair.

"At least we can look out for each other," Zack looked longingly into her stunning blue eyes and smiled as he reached for her hand.

Without thinking Daisy's hand reached for his, before suddenly pausing and pulling away. Even though she could feel something towards him, she didn't quite understand what. Like many of her other friends, Daisy didn't want to rush into things and preferred to take things slow.

Luckily, Zack always looked on the bright side even in the darkest of time which was one of the many things Daisy loved most about him. Time passed by as they chatted away happily to one and another. Daisy could see the love from the sparkle in his eyes every time he spoke to or about her.

Finally, it was 9am and they had already been awake for 3 hours. Now they only had 30 minutes to get ready before they had to greet their new group and see the new horrendous world. Daisy wasn't sure whether she was ready to leave the safe zone but she felt a lot safer in Zack's company.

"I'll let you get ready. We don't have long," Daisy spoke as she started walking out of his room.

"Thanks. Once I'm ready, I'll wait for you outside your room," Zack said.

It took him a few minutes to get dressed as he threw his clothes on. Once finished, Zack stuck to his word and walked along the hallway to wait for Daisy. He waited only five minutes before Daisy came scampering out of her room in her new clothes.

"Hey," she said, staring in astonishment.

Her hair hung loosely over her shoulders as she quickly tied it up into a messy ponytail. She was wearing no jewellery and a black scarf covered in red and pink roses which was wrapped loosely around her neck.

Daisy was also wearing a plain black sleeveless top with a black leather jacket which had thin flexible plastic wrapped around the outside of the sleeves to protect her arms from any zombies that tried to bite or scratch her. Her hands were concealed by long black gloves which had metal on the fingertips and knuckles for more protection

Black tracksuit bottoms covered her legs in order to fully protect her. She had pockets on either side giving her somewhere to put her weapons and a brown belt, tied tightly around her waist. Daisy noticed Zack was staring as she looked down at her new white and black striped trainers.

On the front of her trainers there were short metal spikes which stood out in all directions. They were mostly there in order to give Daisy an advantage over the zombies as she could kick the zombies with them, giving her time to escape.

"Hey," he stuttered, finally managing to say the first word that came to his mind.

Zack was wearing similar clothes to Daisy. He wore a grey camouflage sleeveless top and a dark blue jacket with plastic covering his sleeves too. Grey fingerless gloves showed of his skinny fingers as he tucked the loose strands of hair inside a blood red hat.

Baggy grey jeans covered his legs as they were held up with a red and blue striped belt. On either side of his jeans there was a holster holding two throwing knives. Zack wore the same styled trainers as Daisy but with fewer spikes. His trousers hid part of the trainers, dragging onto the floor as he bent down and tucked them into his shoes.

"Come on let's go. We don't want to be late on the first day! That would be embarrassing." Daisy explained.

Daisy and Zack hurried down loads of different hallways desperately trying to find the way out. They found that some led to nowhere while others led to dark and gloomy rooms which they never wanted to enter again as they were unaware of what was inside, and didn't particularly want to find out. They hastily ran to meet their new co-workers by the main doors of the building.

As they arrived they noticed Adam, was standing by the doors, waiting to unlock all the padlocks. Even though he held a clipboard in his left hand and a pen in his right, he looked more relaxed than when they first met him. Daisy saw a light aqua colour headband, holding his hair in place.

He wore a long light grey top with a long vibrant yellow stripe that went across it diagonally. Adam was also wearing a pair of tight dark grey jeans with no belt but instead he had two holsters; one holding a hand gun and the other one holding a dagger.

"Now that everyone is finally here; I'll hand the register over to Zoe," Adam said, giving the clipboard and pen to her.

"Thank you, sir," Zoe replied, taking it carefully.

"Silence everyone," Adam shouted, "NOW!"

"Lucy, Jade and Jason," Zoe called out.

"Here," they replied.

"James and Emily," Zoe shouted.

"Here," they said in unison.

"They're all here, sir," Zoe, handed the clipboard back over to Adam.

"Thank you," Adam began, "there's three new people joining the group. Daisy, Zack and Cameron please wave."

The trio waved awkwardly as everyone's hawk eyes turned to them, making the three friends feel strange. Daisy gulped as she saw people look at her up and down in disgust as if they were judging her for her looks and clothing. Within a minute, they stopped. turning their heads away from them and back at the leader in synchronised order. Once again they gave him their full attention as if they didn't care about the new arrivals.

"Now; everybody you'll be split into three different groups," Zoe said calmly as Adam coughed before reading the groups out loud.

"Group one is Zack, Daisy, Zoe, Emily and Cameron. You'll be checking outside. Make sure it's safe! Group two is Jason, James and Lucy who'll be checking houses and securing them. Group three is Jade, Tyler and me. We'll be checking the woods as well as setting traps. Is that clear?" Adam explained as he put the clipboard by the door.

"Yes Sir," everyone said.

"Jason, your group will be going first. As soon as those doors open, I want your group to be as quiet as mice and check the coast is clear," Adam said as he unlocked the door, leaning against it.

Jason seized hold of his gun before giving Jade a hug goodbye. Adam slowly opened the door letting Jason quietly tiptoe outside. Nothing but silence surrounded them as James and Lucy followed. Adam peered around the corner before directing his group to leave. Jade and Tyler darted out the door alongside Adam, leaving only one group behind.

"Right guys I know you're new but you have to follow my command. It's kind of important that you listen to me, it's life or death out there. If you think your funny and make one wrong move, you'll be instantly turned into one of those horrible brain dead monsters and of course you definitely don't want that. But only use your guns as a last resort because the loud noise will attract more of them which is why you have a dagger each. Make sure you aim for their heads and nowhere else, if you don't get them in the right spot, you may end up paying the price with your life," Zoe said, opening the door slowly.

"Oh, stop yacking on!" Cameron said confidently, "No one wants to hear you moan and whine. I want to leave already."

"Cameron!" Daisy said in shock.

"How about you shut up, before I make you. I'm in charge now. So if you want to live, I suggest you do everything in your power to keep yourself safe and others protected, along with protecting what's left of our so called village," Zoe responded angrily.

She gave the all clear sign as the four of them followed Zoe outside. Daisy looked around at the sad devastating sight which was once their beloved town where they grew up. Memories flooded back as she remembered running down the high street to go to the candy store and going to the park to play on the swings and slide while scoffing her face with all different kind of sweets.

She thought of the small memories, that she cherished the most, even just walking down the street with a friend. A tear dripped down her face as Daisy quickly wiped it away, making sure no one noticed. She didn't want anyone thinking she was weak, she had to be strong for everyone.

The town had changed so much since it all began. Before, the village was a happy friendly place but now was a paradise for zombies. Buildings were on fire as bright yellow flames burst through the windows, shattering glass onto the ground below. Nearly every car was over turned, smashed or broken into. This wasn't the village they once knew and had all grown up to love; it was now a huge zombie infested dump.

it can affect your lungs and breathing. After I've thrown it run and shoot but stay together. Keep your heads low. I don't want anyone getting harmed from the smoke," Zoe chucked it as everyone covered their mouths and noses, "RUN! And FIRE."

Everyone grabbed their guns, swinging it from their sides as they held onto them tightly before shooting at the zombies. In the far distance they could hear more zombies moaning and they knew more were coming. They had to leave now. However, they didn't know how far the zombies were, or which direction the noises came from. Out of confusion they all started to run in different directions.

Daisy started becoming riddled with worry as they all began separating, and Zack got further and further away from her. Realising no-one knew where to go, they called out, banding together as they moved slowly in one direction.

"RUN!" Zoe shouted, clinging onto Zack's arm.

As zombies got closer, the moans started surrounding them. Back at the hideout Scarlett was beginning to get bored, she didn't like being indoors without any excitement or action, and took it upon herself to leave the base alone.

On the tour of the hideout, they had been shown the weapon room as well as where they kept the extra clothes just in case zombies got in. She decided to sneak off, getting equipped with the right clothing for safety.

It didn't take her too long to get dressed; making sure it was safe but fashionable as she loved to make a statement. Finally, it was time to leave. Running to the main door, she noticed all the locks had been left open, as if it was meant to be her chance. It was like the world was telling her to go. "That was easy," Scarlett thought to herself.

The large door creaked open as her left foot went forward entering the outside world, followed by her right foot. She was shocked that she was finally free. Scarlett took a breath of the frozen fresh air, giving a little evil smile of delight as she walked into the middle of the road. She felt free, unstoppable, like she could do anything. It felt so long since she had stepped outside in to the real world.

It felt like a dream to her but she knew it was real. This was her life now and she was fine with it. She had no parents nagging at her, telling her what to do and no siblings that she had to share her belongings with or be compared to anymore. This was a fresh start for her and everyone else. No more feeling left out or alone.

All of a sudden Scarlett heard a curdling scream as she looked around in shock, seeing nothing but piles of rubbish filling the streets. The sky was grey and moody, creating a disturbing and sinister vibe. Her body automatically twisted around in fear as she tried to figure out what direction it came from. Another scream hollowed around her as she began running towards the sound.

"Finally, something interesting," Scarlett whispered.

Meanwhile; Daisy and her group had heard the same shrieking scream as Scarlett. Daisy and Zack looked around cautiously, at this point they're both worried what they might see. Zoe grabbed her gun, getting ready for a gruesome fight just in case there were more zombies. She carried on walking ignoring the sound, acting as if she never heard a thing.

"Ignore it, that isn't our fight," Zoe said, beginning to walk away as her stomach twisted making her feel ill, trying not to drop on the floor.

"What if it's our people?" Emily asked worriedly.

"We have orders to obey! Those orders do not include following that noise," Zoe said raising her voice.

Emily suddenly went quiet as fear flooded throughout her body, looking stunned. Unexpectedly, a gunshot sound danced through the air as it bounced off each building. It echoed, spreading the noise as everyone listened closely. Zoe and Cameron took no notice of the sound as they began arguing again, causing the group to worry especially Emily, knowing it could attract the dead.

"Please don't raise your voice at her, she's just a child she doesn't understand properly what's going on," Cameron explained, showing his softer side.

"Is anyone going to take any notice of that gunshot, you can't just make us ignore it. What is it? And where did it come from?" Daisy asked, giving Zoe and Cameron a look.

"Sorry but I'm in charge, not you! If someone questions my leadership; I will raise my voice. So deal with it," Zoe answered back.

"No one I'm guessing," Zack replied to Daisy.

"No-one questioned your leadership? She simply asked a question! And what did you do? Tell her off. Setting a good example, aren't you?" Cameron shouted.

"I guess not," Daisy muttered.

"Please stop arguing," Emily begged, stamping her foot angrily, trying to get their attention.

Daisy and Zack looked at Emily as they gestured for her to secretly join them. Emily instantly did as she was told, and was more than happy to get away from Zoe and Cameron who were constantly screaming at each other. Zack knew they had to do something as not knowing where the sound came from or who it belonged to was killing him inside. It was in his nature to help others, even if he didn't know them.

"Yes?" Emily said shyly.

"Daisy and I are going to find out what happened. Can you distract them?" Zack asked.

"If we have any problems we'll contact you over the walkie-talkies," Daisy explained.

"Of course I can. I doubt it will be a problem," Emily folded her arms as she giggled softly before walking to Zoe and Cameron who were still arguing.

"Thank you," Daisy and Zack whispered.

They grabbed hold of their bags, sneaking away, checking that they didn't catch Zoe's attention. Meanwhile, Scarlett ran around the town trying to find the source of the screaming. Not long after she arrived outside a big supermarket and heard a louder scream coming from inside. She had found it.

Shattered glass covered the ground as the doors swung, tiny droplets of blood trailed from the path to inside giving a creepy and eerie vibe. Scarlett could tell something bad had happened in a hurry.

Her hand shook as she reached for the door handle, tightly grasping the knife with her other hand. She switched the lights on, trying to brighten up the darkness. The lights flickered like candles. Stepping inside the building, she noticed more of the damage the apocalypse had done.

"Hello?" Scarlett shouted nervously, "Anyone here?"

Immediately she regretted calling as a humongous ravenous bloodthirsty zombie; covered in blood came gliding round the corner, leaving long gory skid marks behind it. Scarlett screamed as the zombie dived at her face, inches away from her skin wanting to devour her.

She suddenly threw herself onto the floor, desperately rolling away from the zombie's grasp. Thankfully she managed to roll enough, giving her a few extra seconds to reach for her gun. Her shaking fingers clasped at the thin air as she soon came to a realization that her gun had scooted across the room during the struggle of getting away. In fear and regret she shuffled herself backwards on the cold wooden floor, knowing the end was almost near.

Suddenly she shut her eyes, preparing herself to die in the next 20 seconds. A bullet shot through the zombie's torn up head making it drop to the floor in a puddle of its own sticky smelly blood. Scarlett slowly opened her eyes, amazed that she was alive as she saw Daisy and Zack standing beside her with their hands on their hips, tapping their feet irritably at Scarlett for putting herself into danger.

"What the hell Scarlett! You were supposed to stay behind, where it's safe!" Zack shouted angrily.

"I was bored, there was nothing to do. I do need some thrill in my life," Scarlett answered back sarcastically.

The room instantly went quiet as everyone took their time to catch their breath, trying to hold their anger in. Zack couldn't believe how careless Scarlett had been as he saw Daisy hold her hand out for her. He glanced at her as he sighed before putting his hands in his back pockets.

"I don't need your help!" Scarlett moaned.

"You would be dead if it wasn't for us. Where's our thank you!" Zack shouted, his words hissing like a snake.

Scarlett grabbed Daisy's hand before Daisy changed her mind about her kind gesture. She stood up as she looked at the floor, not knowing what to say. Out of nowhere, they suddenly heard a loud moan coming from behind them as they all quickly spun around.

Daisy was standing face to face with a zombie; its jaw gruesomely hung loose off its face, showing its bloody teeth with flesh sewn into the gaps of each tooth as blood trailed down it's shredded chin. She screamed as she tripped, hitting the ground.

It walked forwards leaning over her body, drooling on her face, ready to pounce. Scarlett darted across the room in search of her gun as Zack threw himself in front of Daisy without a second thought, pushing her out of the way. With a terrifying shriek, the zombie dug its rotten teeth into Zack's leg as he screamed in agony.

Daisy froze in fear as she watched the blood squirt out of his leg. The screams echoed through her ears as Scarlett quickly grabbed her gun. Daisy's heart sank to the floor, as the love of her life was dying in front of her eyes. She could feel her blue eyes tearing up ready to spill all over the shop floor. Scarlett held her gun out in front of her as she shot the zombie.

Blood exploded as the bullet sliced through the zombie's head leaving a gaping hole. She felt bad for putting them in danger, knowing if she had never snuck out Daisy and Zack would have had a better chance of coming back alive. Scarlett slowly approached Zack with caution as she raised her gun to his head.

"Wait!" Daisy shouted to Scarlett as she saw the gun to his head, "You can't! You don't know if he'll turn yet!"

Daisy moved closer to Zack until he was lying in front of her in a pool of blood. She slowly and carefully lifted his head onto her lap, stroking his once dark brown hair now drenched in blood. Her hands were soaked in his blood but she didn't care as she took in the last few minutes she had with him.

"I… love you… Daisy," he stuttered

"I love you too Zack, I always will," Daisy answered

"I need to say… Something important," Zack coughed.

Chapter 9
We Should Have Known

His emerald green eyes slowly closed as he drifted in and out of consciousness. A look of worry sprung upon and overpowered Daisy's face as he started trying to gasp for air. Zack looked up at Daisy; his eyes turning a dark moss green as he stared into her beautiful eyes. Grasping hold of her soft hand, he took a long breath in before smiling at her.

Zack knew what he needed to say and he knew it was time for it. He wanted to wait till they were older to be the right time when he asked her. As he lay on his death bed; he knew if he didn't ask her now, he would regret it.

"Will you... be mine" Zack said before going quiet.

No sound managed to escape from his dry mouth as his eyes stared blankly into space, showing no emotion. His last breath gently blew against Daisy's soft warm cheek. A tear slowly dripped down the side of his pale cheek, making it seem like he was crying. Daisy couldn't stand seeing him like this as she lifted her hand over his face and gently closed his eyes for him.

"Zack... I love you!" Daisy said as a tear appeared, making her eyes glisten, falling down her cheek.

Daisy looked at the floor in despair as more tears filled her eyes, making everything blur around her. She didn't want to feel or love ever again, her heart was aching and broken, causing her to feel as if her heart was sinking to the bottom of the deepest part of the ocean. He was her one true love; she had never felt these feelings before and only ever had them for him. Their love was real and pure and now there was nothing. She felt empty.

Scarlett stood by her side, resting her hand on Daisy's shoulder wanting to show support and comfort. She stood up, turned around and hugged Scarlett before letting all her emotions weep out. Freezing in shock, Scarlett didn't know how to react as her arms slowly raised, hugging Daisy back.

While Scarlett comforted Daisy, they realised no one had shot Zack in the head, stopping him from turning. All of a sudden his grey bloody hand shot up from the floor, instantly grabbing Daisy's foot as he left a gory bloody handprint on one of her new trainers. A loud evil moan escaped from his rotting mouth as she saw his mossy green eyes fading into a bright yellow, that lit up his dark ashy skin.

Daisy panicked, freezing right before him. He was covered in blood as his dead mouth dropped open ready to bite her, trying to turn her into an undead corpse like him. His yellow teeth showing as he began drooling. She wasn't sure if she could live in a world without him but before she knew it, Scarlett had pulled her away as she raised her gun towards his head. Daisy turned around, not wanting to see it as she heard a gun fire echo through the building.

"Nooooooooo," Daisy cried, collapsing to her knees falling onto the floor.

In her mind she knew it was the right thing to do by letting him go, but deep in her heart she didn't want to accept that he's gone. She couldn't take it upon herself to look behind her as she knew it would destroy her mentally and physically. Even though she wanted to believe that the new world was worth living in, however she was no longer sure about it. Could she really go on living without Zack? Scarlett gently tucked her gun away as she looked over at Daisy.

"I'm so sorry Daisy. I had to shoot him, he would have devoured you. We really must go now, the noise will attract more of them," Scarlett explained as she held her hand out the same way as Daisy had done for her.

Scarlett left Daisy standing alone as she dragged Zack's lifeless body and cramped it into a broom cupboard leaving a gruesome trail of dead skin and clotted blood. She didn't want Daisy to suffer any more than she had to. Taking one last glance, she shut the door as she took a long deep breath in. Suddenly she turned around as she heard a squeak of a shoe.

To her surprise, she saw a small girl with long light blonde hair in a messy plait with sticks and leaves standing out of it. The girl stared at her with wide eyes as if she saw a ghost. She looked no older than 10 years old and was clutching tightly onto an old scruffy ragdoll, not wanting to let it go.

Her red cheeks were dampened with tears and her young eyes were bright red, bloodshot and puffy. She wore a purple striped top, covered in rips and fresh mud, looking as if she had just run through a field of brambles. She wore navy blue leggings with thorns attached to it and pink trainers with a little raven on the heels. Around her neck she wore a small silver heart locket.

"Please can you help me, I don't know what to do," the little girl cried, "I'm Abigail, I've lost my older sister."

Before Scarlett could reply, they heard people banging on what was left of the windows as Jade, Tyler and Adam rushed in. They were all out of breath, gasping for air. Abigail ran over to Scarlett, hiding behind her, looking frightened as they all stood in front of them.

"What's happened?" Scarlett asked confused.

"Why are you here? Never mind, we don't have time. The village is overrun with zombies," Tyler shouted.

He took his cold water bottle out of his bag, gulping it down. Without warning; Lucy, Jason and James dropped out of a ventilation shaft onto the ground, everyone jumped out of the way. The deafening sound pierced through the empty shopping centre as they heard a faint moan.

Lucy stood up frantically clutching her shoulder in pain as she held her breath. She could see part of the bone looking dislocated as she slammed her shoulder against the wall, locking it back in place. A loud scream diverted their eyes to her as her face went pale, still holding her shoulder.

"Are you okay?" Jade said, rushing over with Tyler and Adam to help.

"There are too many," Lucy explained, "We're not going to make it!"

"I've got two questions," Adam said looking puzzled, "Who's the kid and where's Zack?"

Scarlett glanced at Daisy who was sitting in the corner by herself as she quietly sobbed alone. With the memories of Zack overflowing her mind with mixed emotions; she would never forget the look in his eyes as he died, trying to save her. Using his last words as he took his final breath.

Thankfully she never saw his facial expression as Scarlett shot him dead but the sound still haunted her mind. She stared at the floor in a daze, feeling sick to her stomach as his last words floated around her mind. Her thoughts finally stopped, pulling her back into reality as she heard a massive crash.

The main door to the shopping centre had smashed, shattering shards of glass across the cold floor. They couldn't see what had happened but they could hear it as they froze, staring at each other. Adam cautiously walked around the corner, knowing it could be his last moment on this earth but he was ready to fight with everything he had.

A few seconds later he ran back, screaming with all the air he had in his lungs, as a large crowd of zombies fled after him wanting to eat his brain. They were only a few inches away from him but he wasn't giving up, he carried on running as he suddenly shouted a certain word at his group.

"RUN!" Adam shouted.

Grabbing hold of Abigail's hand, Scarlett rushed over to Daisy as she caught hold of her arm and ran off with them without looking back. Everyone screamed as they fled the scene in terror, making it clear that they only cared about themselves, running off in different directions.

Unfortunately, Lucy was running and too busy looking behind her to notice she was heading into a hoard of flesh eating zombies. Her ear-shrieking scream filled the room as the hoard of the undead pounced on her. With the pressure of hundreds of dead bodies falling upon her, she collapsed as they clawed at her pale flesh. Ripping layer by layer off, she bled out on the floor in agony.

Suddenly another pack of newly turned zombies twisted their bodies around, their bones clicking as they spun facing

Scarlett, Daisy and Abigail with their freshly torn up faces. The three of them were huddling closely together as they cowered in a darkened corner. The zombies stumbled, getting closer and closer as they surrounded the girls.

Adam looked over at them, noticing the horror on little Abigail's face. He looked around and saw a hand rail hanging loosely of the wall. Without a second thought, he grabbed hold it, yanking it off its hinges before letting it drop and roll across the floor. The sound bellowed like thunder causing the zombies to limp towards him, giving Scarlett, Daisy and Abigail a chance to run for their lives.

Every one scurried for the fire exit, running outside and leaving the building. They watched as Adam barged his way through the zombie hoard but everyone knew that he wouldn't make it. Daisy covered Abigail's eyes, not wanting to ruin her innocent young life with what was about to happen to Adam.

Even though Adam had tried his hardest to escape, he was now surrounded as the zombie hoard overpowered him. A large zombie grabbed at his shirt collar as he pulled away, trying to escape. Unfortunately, more zombies approached as they each grabbed different parts of his body, slamming him to the floor. They began tearing him apart like a pack of wild animals.

His hand reached into the air drenched in fresh blood which was running down his arm. Zombies grabbed him as they sunk their rotten teeth in, leaving a few of their teeth embedded in his skin. Another zombie snarled before yanking at his arm and ripping it off. From all the blood he had lost, he was now dead at least he couldn't suffer anymore.

Zoe, Cameron and Emily arrived, staring silently at the scene in shock as they saw his dead body lying still, covered in blood. His intestines were hanging loosely out of his stomach, but as they looked up they saw all the zombies staring back at them hungrily. They turned around, noticing everyone else was running away.

Without thinking, Zoe ran after them as Cameron and Emily quickly followed. The zombies were starting to gather more of the undead, banding together as they began chasing the living. Separating from the group; Abigail, Daisy and Scarlett disappeared as they ran down a long thin alley way and jumped behind some bins, to hide.

Noticing a café door slightly ajar, Jade and Tyler darted inside as they held it open for Jason and James. With them all safe inside, Jade closed the doors and locked it. They ran round the counter and hid behind it, letting Tyler peek over in order to check they were safe.

Zoe and Cameron ran back to the hideout unaware that Emily was standing alone in the middle of the road. Fear rushed through her body as she looked around trying to find a familiar face, a scream escaped her mouth as the zombies got closer. Scarlett quickly ran into the open, grabbing hold of her before pulling her into the alleyway where they were hiding. Emily hugged her tightly, too scared to let go.

"Emily you have to be quiet," Scarlett whispered.

Emily nodded, taking a few deep breaths in as she tried to control her breathing. Abigail immediately recognised the alleyway as she tugged at the door handle behind them trying to open it. Unfortunately, it was locked.

"What are you doing?" Daisy asked.

"It's my dad's old house," Abigail replied, "There's a spare key under the bins as he always loses his."

Daisy and Scarlett quickly lifted the bins together as Abigail stood out of the way. Emily crawled underneath in search for the key. She noticed something shimmering at the back as she reached for it.

"Got it," she shouted joyfully, sliding out from underneath the bins.

"Be quiet," Scarlett hissed, helping her up.

Abigail snatched the key from Emily's tiny hands, rushing to unlock the door. Emily looked behind her, hearing a small moan as she saw zombies at either end of the alleyway, realising they were trapped. She turned around about to warn her friends as the undead walked speedily towards them.

"Please hurry up," Emily begged.

With a twist of the key, the door unlocked as Abigail turned the handle. She carefully opened it before entering with

Scarlett and Daisy following, holding their guns out at the ready in order to protect themselves. Emily stood outside and was suddenly yanked in before closing the door.

The house was giving off a very homely vibe as family photos hung loosely on the rainbow coloured walls. There were old grey coloured furniture covered in dust and cat fur, the pillows were covered in stains as were the carpets. It didn't look like anyone had lived here in a while as they brushed the cobwebs out of their way.

"Who did you live with?" Daisy asked.

"My parents and my older sister Jessica," Abigail replied as they all went quiet, hearing a movement from upstairs.

Scarlett carefully climbed the stairs, ensuring she didn't make a sound as Abigail, Emily and Daisy trailed behind her. All of a sudden a young lady about 15 years old jumped out from behind a door, at the top of the stairs, holding a tennis racket. She had long brown hair tucked behind her ears letting everyone see her light brown eyes and the fear that was on her face.

Even though they were in an apocalypse, she looked as if she'd looked after herself very well and was wearing a dark purple top hidden by a light green hoody. Blue pre-ripped jeans covered her skinny legs. Abigail stared at her for a few seconds, letting her eyes focus on her. She ran towards her, barging Scarlett out of her way, she sobbed, giving her a massive hug.

"Jessica," Abigail said in delight, "You scared us!"

"You made me jump," Jessica replied, wrapping her arms tightly around her little sister, "Who are they?"

Abigail introduced the group to her sister, explaining how they had saved her. Scarlett and Daisy tucked their guns back into their pockets as they all nervously waved at her. Jessica smiled back before looking at Abigail, thankful for what they had done for her little sister.

"Where's mum and dad?" Abigail asked.

"They went out looking for you!" Jessica explained, "I haven't seen them since."

Chapter 10
Burning Hell

"Oh," Abigail said, her lips quivering.

Without warning the windows by the back door shattered as they heard heavy footsteps getting louder. Abigail shuddered, looking up at her friends and Jessica before hiding behind them. A plate smashed as they heard chairs being knocked over.

"Wait here," Scarlett demanded.

Jessica pulled Abigail and Emily into her room, closing the door in order to keep them safe. She gripped her tennis racket tighter as Daisy and Scarlett lifted their guns ready to shoot, carefully tiptoeing down the uneven stairs.

They entered the kitchen, looking at the back door before quickly ducking under a wooden table covered with a white cloth. Scarlett stared at the floor. There was a rock, surrounded by shards of broken glass. Looking up, she saw blood dripping from the window frame.

Daisy's eyes darted around the kitchen as they stopped, seeing a zombie lying on the floor. A knife stuck out directly in the middle of its head with blood slowly dripping, leaving a gruesome puddle underneath its rotting corpse. She saw its raw skin with maggots crawling out, trying to wriggle free. Its skin was slowly turning pale red as the zombie twitched one last time before lying still.

Cameron and Zoe stood behind the zombie with blood splatters covering their clothes and faces. Grabbing her knife, Zoe yanked it out of the zombie's brain as she wiped the blood onto its clothes. Suddenly they screamed as the table wobbled. They hugged each other as fear rushed through their bodies.

Zoe suddenly pushed him away as she saw two shadows appearing. Without warning Zoe chucked her knife, throwing it inches away from Scarlett's foot which was peeping out from underneath the table. Scarlett and Daisy crawled out, putting their arms up in the air as they stood up.

"Watch it!" Scarlett yelled, walking towards them.

"Are you serious?!?" Cameron shouted, stepping away from Zoe, "It's just you two!"

"Oh Cam, were you scared?" Zoe asked, beginning to laugh.

"Me! You were the one that screamed. Scaredy-cat," Cameron explained, crossing his arms.

"As if. I never screamed and I am definitely not a scaredy-cat," Zoe said, crossing her arms too as she turned her back to face away from him.

"Shut up you two. You were both scared," Scarlett interrupted.

"We were not," Cameron and Zoe said in unison.

For the first time they actually agreed on something. They looked at each other angrily as Zoe raised her eyebrows crossly. Cameron shook his head as his blood boiled with hatred. Even though they had agreed on one thing, they still couldn't get past their weird but unique friendship.

"You two would make such a cute couple," Daisy laughed.

"Yuck," they both said at the same time.

Once again they looked at each other but this time a smirk appeared on both of their faces. They unfolded their arms as they let them drop to their sides. Emily, Jessica and Abigail arrived in the kitchen as Cameron and Zoe stared at Jessica weirdly.

"Care to explain, who the new girl is?" Zoe asked, pointing at Jessica.

"That's my sister Jessica," Abigail explained as she gave her a hug.

"Okay," Zoe replied, "Anyway we will be staying here tonight as its 8:30pm and already dark. We don't want to be caught outside with the zombies."

"No need to ask," Jessica said sarcastically as Zoe dumped her bag on the floor before kicking her shoes off.

"Where do you keep the extra blankets?" Zoe asked ignoring Jessica's remark.

"In the cupboard in the lounge," Abigail explained as she pointed her in the right direction.

Zoe rushed to the lounge, grabbing some extra blankets before handing them out. Eventually they all found a place to sleep. It took them a while to doze off but soon enough they were all fast asleep in their own dream lands.

The next morning, they were woken up abruptly to screaming. Everyone followed the sound, they saw the windows by the leather sofa had been smashed as broken glass laid shattered everywhere. The cream coloured curtains were ripped and there were drops of blood covering the windowsill.

Cameron was lying on the sofa with a zombie pinning him down. His arms were out stretched, holding the zombie back as its jaw snapped trying to catch a bite of Cameron's flesh. He yelled as he raised his leg, kicking it in its chest, not leaving a single mark. The zombie slipped off the sofa, grabbing Cameron's foot as it fell to the floor.

"HELP!" He screamed with his back against the sofa, "Anyone?"

The zombie scuttled like a cockroach towards him as he shuffled backwards, pulling his knees into his chest in fear of his life. His head snuggled tightly between his knees as he gently rocked himself back and forth. While Cameron was terrified, the zombie was dragging its blood covered body across the floor, nearly at his feet.

As he looked up he caught the sight of Zoe with Daisy and Scarlett standing behind her. His face lightened up as he pushed himself further against the sofa. Jessica darted in leaving Emily and Abigail standing speechless in the doorway.

"Don't just stand there, help me," He screamed.

Jessica ran past Zoe, holding the tennis racket by her side as she snuck up behind the zombie, whacking it with all her strength on its head. The zombie quickly turned around, forgetting about Cameron as it crawled towards her. Once again she hit it but this time the tennis racket broke so she threw it to the side. She walked backwards, feeling defenceless as another zombie climbed through the broken window. It grabbed hold of Jessica's long brown hair.

"HELP," she screamed as a few more zombies clambered through the window.

Zoe, Daisy and Scarlett grabbed their guns as they started shooting at the zombies. Emily and Abigail stood still, frozen in fear, watching each bullet pierce the zombie's stomachs as they flew out of the other side, with blood gushing out.

Even though the zombies were losing a great amount of blood, they were acting as if they felt nothing. With one last bullet each, they aimed for the heads of the zombies as they pulled the trigger. The zombies collapsed to the floor in a pool of their own sticky grim blood.

Daisy dropped her gun in shock, remembering the same sound that had killed Zack. Scarlett and Emily walked over to Cameron as they saw blood soak through his shirt. Without saying a word, Emily hastily exited the room before arriving back with two towels and a bandage.

All of a sudden; Jessica's breathing got slower as she felt a large heavy pain weigh down on her chest. She fell against the sofa and her face grew paler. Her hazel eyes were open slightly as she looked around in a panic. Her hands started shaking as they began to sweat.

"What's happening?" Zoe asked, "I didn't think the zombie bit her."

"She didn't get bitten. It's a panic attack. She always gets them but don't worry, it doesn't last long. All I need to do is calm her down and she'll be fine," Abigail explained.

She hastily walked over to her sister as she bent down beside her. Zoe had never seen someone have a panic attack before, her eyes glued to Jessica and Abigail as she observed very carefully. Scarlett and Emily carried on helping Cameron as they cautiously lifted his shirt up. They noticed a piece of broken glass sticking out of his stomach, removing it before bandaging up his wound.

"Deep breath Jess, you'll be okay. Just breath, in and out. That's it," Abigail said, comforting her sister.

After a few minutes of listening to Abigail's soothing voice, Jessica had returned back to normal. Her hands were still shaking slightly from the shock but her colour was slowly returning to her face as Jessica took a long deep breath in.

"Well done. Feel better now?" Abigail said.

"Yes. I'm fine," Jessica answered quietly as she looked up at Abigail who was extremely worried.

Abigail rolled her eyes as Jessica stood up in a rush, walking over to the kitchen to grab her handbag from the coat hanger. She hurriedly shoved all of her important items into the bag including a heart locket similar to her sisters.

"What are you doing?" Abigail asked.

"This place isn't safe anymore, we need to go!" Jessica answered.

"We can go back to the hideout. It's safe and got food and beds," Zoe said as she entered the kitchen.

"Let's go," Daisy shouted through the house at them.

The seven friends tiptoed quietly to the door. Daisy gently pushed it open, letting the hinges creak as she took a step outside. With no zombies in sight Scarlett followed Daisy outside, looking alert as she gestured everyone to follow them.

Zoe looked at them with a disapproved look spread across her face as she thought about Adam's sacrifice to save all of them. Now he was gone, she could finally take charge and be the boss of everyone. They would have to do what she said, when she said it or leave and find somewhere else.

She barged past Abigail and Jessica, pushing Emily out of her way too before knocking into Cameron. Zoe stood in the doorway, arms stretched blocking the exit. Scarlett and Daisy looked at her, waiting for her to speak.

"Who put you two in charge?" Zoe questioned them, "The leader might have died but that doesn't mean the rules have changed!"

"That's it; I've had it with you! Since we've arrived, you've acted as if we're the monsters. We're not the real threat, those creatures are!" Daisy shouted angrily.

"Don't you dare talk to me like that!" Zoe yelled.

"Why not? You've been treating us like that," Scarlett replied.

"Have I?" she asked in an almost whisper tone.

Everyone nodded apart from Jessica who hardly knew Zoe or any of them. Zoe was speechless as she stood frozen to the ground, finally realising her actions had been wrong and unfair. She had lost her sense of way when the apocalypse started.

"Scarlett you can lead, I'll take a step back and go in the middle," Zoe explained as she smiled politely.

"Thank you Zoe. Daisy can you go at the back as you also have a gun. Emily and Cameron you two will go behind me. Abigail and Jessica behind Zoe. Is everyone ready?" Scarlett explained.

They scuttled their way through the alleyway, dodging every zombie they saw as they hid behind any obstacles they could, out of their sight. The group carried on walking to the end of the alley as they began rapidly moving in the direction of their hideout.

The town was quiet with no zombies rustling around. Buildings were empty with shattered glass still lying untouched covered in blood on the ground. Rain started washing it away as it cleaned the streets that looked like they belonged in hell.

A massive smoke filled cloud surrounded the sky as they ran, following the smoke, which lead back to their hideout. Blasting hot fiery flames danced in all directions as the smoke consumed the house within its deathly fumes. The scene was horrifying as they heard screams of people in pain. Zoe ran towards the building as Jessica grabbed her.

"What are you doing?" Zoe asked.

"You'll die, if you go in there," Jessica explained.

"I don't care. Someone has to help them. I'm the secondary leader, so don't try and stop me!" Zoe shouted, "Now let me go!"

Zoe pushed her away, using all her force as Jessica fell to the ground. Seizing her chance, Zoe ran into the burning building without a second thought. All they heard was screaming and coughing for a few seconds and then it went quiet with only the sound from the crackling of the fire eating away at the building. Daisy suddenly realised her brother Josh had been inside there along with everyone else. She couldn't bear to lose anyone else, not after losing Zack.

"Josh!" Daisy shouted as she ran to the burning building.

A young man suddenly grabbed her arm, pulling her backwards. As she turned around she saw Brianna and her brother Josh standing before her stinking of the smoke. She gave him a massive hug, her eyes filling with tears as she sobbed in his arms. Daisy was so happy he was alive and couldn't hold her tears back anymore.

Ten people swiftly appeared behind, they were holding their guns out at them. They looked at Daisy and her friends who stood still, unsure of what to do as none of them had been in a situation like this before.

Chapter 11
We Should Have Known Better

"Are you infected," a man with black hair shouted as he gripped his gun tighter.

Josh stepped in front of Daisy, wanting to protect his family as he knew these people weren't to be messed with. Jessica held Abigail's hand, giving it a little squeeze trying to comfort her as Emily quickly hid behind Scarlett and Cameron.

"Answer us! Are you infected or not?" Someone else shouted.

"No," Cameron replied.

"That's good," one of the younger men said.

"At least we don't have to kill anyone yet," a lady whispered to the man.

The unknown group of people darted towards Daisy and her group, keeping a close eye on them from a distance. Half of the new group were still holding their guns firmly ready to shoot as if they were expecting them to fight back. Daisy looked at her brother as they started getting closer.

Josh stepped forwards, stopping the new group from getting any closer. Something didn't feel right with them, he wasn't sure what but he knew his instincts had never failed him before. He stood between the groups as a lady from the other group pushed her way through.

She wore an army camouflaged jacket with loose black trousers. He could see that her greenish blue eyes were hiding a secret as she flicked her ginger shoulder length hair out of her face, so Josh could see her better.

"Josh?" the young lady said.

"Caitlyn, is that you?" Josh asked.

"Guys it's okay, I know them," Caitlyn answered as she gave Josh a little smile.

Everyone watched the smouldering flames consume the building as they saw the once beautiful ivy covered building turn to ash. Caitlyn turned her head; looking at the last survivors of the safe zone, they reminded her that the building had once stood tall but now crumbling before them.

A faint voice shouted from behind them as they swiftly turned around. Lewis sprinted out of the building clutching Lindsey in his arms. His blonde hair was darkened with smoke and ash, hiding his freckled face. Within seconds they stood beside Lindsey and Lewis.

Two more faces appeared as Emily walked out from behind Scarlett, recognising the boy as Jake. She ran towards him with her arms outstretched, ready to give him a massive hug. Cameron followed her, recognising his sister who was clutching hold of someone for support.

"Lindsey," Cameron shouted joyfully.

"Jake," Emily said in tears.

Lindsey's eyes were swollen shut with her face enclosed in cuts and bruises. Ash covered her entire body, hiding her inflamed rouge lips. Lewis's legs suddenly gave in as he collapsed. Cameron swiftly picked up Lindsey into his arms as Lewis hit the ground.

"I'm Sorry. I don't know what happened," Lewis whispered, "There were too many zombies. There was fire everywhere. Everyone was dying. I couldn't do anything."

A tear dropped down his tender reddened cheek. Two large men and a petite lady hurried over to Lewis and Lindsey, quickly checking their pulse. Lewis's face sunk as he explained about the fire, remembering every detail.

"It happened so fast! Someone had invaded the zone. They lit a candle and threw a towel on top of it, letting the fire spread. We only saw them for a few seconds as everyone started panicking. Zombies fled through the broken doors. Suddenly the fire absorbed the corridors. I saw Lindsey lying on the floor, I couldn't leave her, so I helped her and escaped," Lewis explained.

"What happened to Amy?" Scarlett asked as she gulped, knowing the outcome, "Is she?"

"Yes... She's dead," Lewis looked down at the ground in dismay.

"Oh," Scarlett said as she felt her throat tighten.

"She'll be fine, she just needs to rest," a tall man said from Caitlyn's group.

"We'd better get going. If we stay here any longer, there's a chance we'll probably end up dead," one of the guys said.

"Jacob's right," Caitlyn replied to the man with black hair from her group, "everyone please follow us."

Without a second thought; they followed Caitlyn and her group, not knowing where they were going to end up. It was a short journey but they finally arrived at an underground car park. Darkness surrounded them as a cold wind blew past the cars, brushing against their faces.

Everyone held their guns firmly once again as they walked further into the car park, watching their every step. Shadows were lurking in every corner as growls echoed through the darkness. They huddled close together as they carried on walking past the flickering lights that were built into the ceiling.

All of a sudden a small shadow swiftly moved behind them as they twisted around. Holding their guns in front of them, they slowly approached it as a little Jack Russell dog ran towards them. Its bark grew louder with every step it took. Its light brown pointy ears were flat against its small head with its short stump of a tail between its legs.

A taller figure galloped after it, moaning and shouting. As the figure got closer to them; they noticed it wasn't a human, it was a zombie wanting to eat it. One of its arms were hanging loosely of its body, clutching onto a thin piece of bone. Blood slowly dripped down as the dog rapidly jumped into Daisy's arms, still barking loudly.

Zombies were gathering at the scene as the little dog continued barking, making everyone worried. Daisy held it in her arms, trying to calm it down but nothing seemed to work. With the flesh eating creatures slowly approaching, someone swiftly shot it dead, attracting more of them as it echoed through the car park.

Hundreds of zombies ran towards them, pushing past each other as they bumped against the cars, setting alarms off. The noise bellowed as they covered their ears, not knowing what to do next. They were surrounded.

A pair of van lights suddenly turned on making them all jump as it drove towards them, hitting all of the zombies which were in the way, their bodies splitting in half, allowing blood to squirt out.

"Get in," a voice shouted from the van.

They stared at each other as they looked back at the zombies before running to the van. Josh swiftly pulled the back doors open, letting everyone quickly scramble to get in. They jumped in as a rotting hand yanked at Daisy's arm trying to pull her out.

She screamed as she clung tightly on to Scarlett's hand, not wanting to let go and be turned into one of them. The dog looked up at Daisy as it saw her in danger. It snarled, showing its teeth, arching its back, wanting to protect her. Once again Daisy screamed as Scarlett tried with all of her strength to pull her inside. The dog looked up at them before diving for the zombie's arm, sinking its sharp teeth into its rotting flesh.

The zombies grip loosened as Scarlett and Josh quickly grabbed her by the arm, pulling her safely inside. Daisy watched as the dog jumped onto the zombie's back, biting it again as it defended Daisy. The zombie turned around rapidly, as it threw the dog of its back.

It hit the wall as it moaned in pain. More zombies rushed towards it as they pounced on top of the dog. Daisy covered her ears as Scarlett turned her around to block the view. The dog had saved her but had died doing it.

Josh and Caitlyn slammed the van doors shut as it started moving. The driver didn't dodge any of the zombies as she headed straight for them, hitting any that were in the way.

Everyone sat silently still on the van floor till Caitlyn broke the silence.

"I forgot to introduce the team," Caitlyn said, "The two boys in the corner with black hair are Callum and Jacob. They're brothers."

"I'm the oldest, I'm 26 and he's 24," Jacob explained.

"The girl with the short brown hair is Paige," Caitlyn continued, "The girl with the long red wavy hair is Sasha and the other girl, with short blonde hair, is Phoebe…"

"I'm 24. Sasha is 17. Paige is 16. I'm the oldest," Phoebe explained.

"I'm Reece, I'm 17 and that's Dan next to me. He's 18," Reece said.

"Suzey is our driver and she's 28. Aaron is in the passenger seat next to her and he's 21," Caitlyn said.

"I'm guessing you're all tired. You're safe here. Why don't you go to sleep?" Sasha asked.

Josh looked uncertain as she spoke. He didn't want to sleep, knowing that he was leaving them unguarded but he felt so tired that he felt dizzy. He couldn't fight the urge to stay awake anymore as the first of their group fell asleep.

After a long drive, they had finally left the zombie infested village behind. A few of them stood up; looking out the windows at the outside world, watching the fire destroy everything that they had once known. Exhausted and horrified from what they had previously experienced, Daisy and her friends started to fall asleep.

Scarlett's head snuggled against Jake's chest as both of them held each other's hands, not wanting to ever let go. Jake moved his other hand, gently stroking Scarlett's long colourful hair, till they both fell asleep. Daisy curled up into a ball with her legs tucked into her neck as she shivered, trying to stay warm. Her brother was sound asleep as he lay a few feet away from her with his body flat on the floor.

Emily, Abigail and Jessica had fallen asleep sitting up against the side of the van. Abigail slowly slipped, her head landed of her sister's lap as neither of them woke. Lindsey and Cameron slept next to each other as Brianna slept all by herself in the far corner.

"Are they asleep?" Aaron asked.

"I think so," Paige replied, poking Cameron in his side.

"Yes they are!" Sasha said, nudging Paige to stop her from waking Cameron up.

"Are you sure they're asleep?" Suzey asked, "We don't want our plan to be ruined."

"Well if they aren't asleep, then they're dead but as I can see them breathing, they're definitely sleeping," Jacob laughed.

He flicked his black hair out of his skinny freckled face as he folded his arms, trying to relax. Callum sat down next to Dan as he searched through his bag looking for rope. Seizing hold of it, he gave Dan a nervous look as he handed it over to him.

"Are we really going to tie them up and leave them?" Callum asked.

"Yes we are," Dan answered.

"Why?" Caitlyn questioned.

"Think about it, would you? If they find out that we were the reason that their safe zone burned down, what do you think they'll do to us? Do you think they'll let us live after everything they've lost?" Reece asked.

"Maybe they'll be fine about it. I know Josh, he's not the kind of person to hold a grudge," Caitlyn replied, hoping for the best.

"You did know him, he might have changed for all you know," Suzey interrupted.

"Stop dreaming Cait! We live in a world where everyone kills each other or dies trying. This isn't the same world as you use to know. Just remember who saved you, when the apocalypse started," Reece answered.

Caitlyn stared at Josh and Daisy, knowing how much they meant to each other. Every day Josh was away fighting, he never stopped talking about his sister and how he couldn't wait to get back to her.

Realising she couldn't go through with their crazy plan, she started thinking of her own to save her new friends. Her group might have saved her once but Josh had saved her a numerous amount of times when they were away during the war. She felt as if she owed him, the least she could do was save him and his friends.

Phoebe could see the look on Caitlyn's face as she nudged Paige and Sasha. The three of them smirked, knowing Caitlyn would never go through with the plan. Dan passed a book over to Sasha as she passed it to Phoebe. Raising the book, she battered Caitlyn hard on the head. Caitlyn fell sideways as she smacked her face on the van floor, knocking herself unconscious.

Darkness surrounded Caitlyn's bruised eyes as blood slowly dripped out of the fresh cut on her face. She heard whispers circling around her, feeling as if she was being laughed at. She felt betrayed and lonely as a high pitch sound screamed through her ears before everything went silent.

Chapter 12
The Betrayal

They were woken up by a loud crash as they suddenly sat up alert, ready to take on the world once more. It was silent... too silent. The van came to a halt as they noticed everyone from the other group apart from Caitlyn had left.

"Where are they Caitlyn?" Lewis screamed at her, not wanting to trust a word she said.

"We trusted you," Scarlett said.

"I was left behind with you lot because I couldn't go through with their plan," Caitlyn explained.

"Plan... What plan?" Scarlett asked.

All of a sudden the air turned thick with greyish black smoke that suffocated their lungs. Everyone rushed to open the back doors of the van as they began choking on the smoke filled air. Within seconds, the air got too much as they collapsed.

A bright light shone through the windows as the doors to van opened. Daisy and her friends were blinded by the light as they saw shadows lurking over them. Their eyes slowly shut, their heads dropped as they lay on the van floor, not moving

Even though they still couldn't see anything apart from darkness and outlines of the mysterious figures, they were still prepared to fight for their lives. There was a faint smell of smoke in the air which seemed to be slowly dissipating. The shadowed figures quietly whispered between themselves.

A dozen hands carefully lifted them up, one by one, into their arms as they carried them cautiously out of the van. A hand seized Scarlett by her side, making her jump as she screamed. Pain instantly shot through her throat as she gasped for fresh air. Someone took her by her arm, dragging her out of the van as she tried to fight them with all her strength.

A deafening scream made them feel even more unsettled as the unknown figures gripped them tighter, cradling them carefully in their arms. Soon they felt like they were flying as they knew who ever was carrying them was running from something but they didn't know what.

Scarlett threw herself to the ground. She crawled on her hands and knees for a few seconds as her body throbbed with pain. Scarlett tried to get up as her exhausted body went limp, giving in as she fell flat on the ground. She collapsed feeling tired and hopeless.

Her eye sight was still partially blurred as she heard faint noises behind her. Once again she tried to stand but she couldn't; she was too weak and hungry. She saw an outline of a hand reach for her arm as she swiped it away in fear.

"Will you please stop, I'm trying to help you," a male voice said.

Scarlett stopped struggling, letting the person pull her up off the ground. She saw faint outlines of a cliff with fresh long wavy grass surrounding it but nothing else. She had no choice but to trust the stranger who seemed to have his heart in the right place, as far as she knew.

The two of them sighed in relief as they ran after their friends. The smoke had finally cleared; leaving a clear atmosphere behind as everyone took a deep breath of fresh air in. At last they could finally stop as they weren't being chased anymore. Everyone relaxed as Daisy and her friends were lowered onto the ground, letting them rest for a while.

"Are you okay Daisy?" Scarlett asked as Daisy tried to open her eyes.

"Yes. What happened?" Daisy replied.

"We were betrayed by Caitlyn's old friends," Scarlett explained.

"Of course we were. It makes perfect sense as none of them are here," Daisy answered.

There were two girls and six guys within the new group. One of the new guys looked around as he lay back on the long spiky grass to relax, knowing that he had helped someone who had needed it. The girl sitting next to him glanced in his direction.

She opened her mouth as if she was about to say something but the guy quickly sat up, nudging her in the arm to shut her up. She instantly did as she was told, shutting her mouth as she shrugged her shoulders along with the rest of her group.

"I'm Kai and this is Kia!" Kai explained, "This is a small part of our group."

Both of them looked as if they had just come out of school, not like they had been living in a zombie infested world. Kai had black out of control hair. He was wearing a white buttoned top covered by a green hoody with black school trousers that dangled past his ankles, partially covering his trainers. He had no cuts on his skin while Kia had a cut on her knee.

Kia had long brown hair tied up in a ponytail completely showing her face, letting her freckles stand out. She was still wearing her school clothes; a grey jumper which hid her shirt underneath and a green blazer with a small pin attached to it over the top with a pleated black skirt that hung just above her knees.

Scarlett looked around, noticing that others were missing as she ignored what Kai had said, not paying attention to them. Brianna, Jake and Lindsey were missing as well as the group that had betrayed them. Everyone else was sat on the ground with the strangers that had saved their lives. Daisy stared at Scarlett who was watching Emily.

"Where's my brother? Where's Jake?" Emily said in a panic.

Scarlett looked over at the strangers as she thought about the only thing that could have happened to him. After all they were trapped in a van that was filled with smoke which was suffocating them, nearly killing them all. Thankfully most of them were rescued in time but a few of them didn't make it and Scarlett knew Jake was one of them.

"He was wearing a dark blue top with black stripes on the cuffs of his sleeves. He has a rose drawn on his wrist," Emily continued, begging for answers.

"He's the guy with the brown spiky hair and eyes that sparkled like stars," Scarlett explained as she remembered him.

Feeling devastated; he looked over at Kia who quickly walked away, not wanting to be around when he told them the bad news. Scarlett wrapped her arms around Emily's shoulder, knowing what he was about to say. She had to be strong now for Emily's sake and felt as if Emily should never have had to deal with a loss like this especially at her age.

"He's dead," Kai answered, looking at the floor with a heart-breaking expression across his face.

Emily's face suddenly dropped as her bottom lip began quivering with sadness. Her eyes filled with tears as Scarlett's arms tightened, giving her a supportive hug. She wanted to cry with her but didn't want to make Emily feel worse.

"Where's the rest of my group? Brianna and Lindsey?" Daisy asked.

"They also didn't make it," Kai explained.

"There were about nine others but they were the reason the fire started. They tied the van doors shut with rope and left a match lit inside," Kia said in a shy voice.

Kai looked at Kia in shock as he didn't want them to know just yet. He wanted them to know at the right time and he didn't think it was the time for it. They had almost died and they had lost some of their friends as well as finding new ones. It was too late now, they knew who had done it and he was hoping they weren't going to revenge their friend's death.

"Kia!" Kai shouted as he frowned at her.

"Kai!" Kia replied.

"Are you two siblings or something?" Caitlyn said as she looked at Kai and Kia with a confused look.

"No way! She's my neighbour not my sister. We've lived next door to each other for a long time, so I guess she's like a sister to me," Kai answered, "We don't even look alike, I hope not anyway."

"He's too bossy and annoying to be my brother," Kia said shyly, "I'm only 14 and he's 16. Also I don't even have a brother; I only have a sister, thankfully."

Caitlyn and Scarlett laughed at Kia's response as Kai didn't look too impressed. They did look very similar; mainly because they had the same shape faces, apart from that they didn't look like they were related at all. Even their hair and eye colours were different.

Kai lent back down, lying on the grass as he put his hands behind his head. Kia shivered. She stood up, walking over to Caitlyn as she knelt beside her and started chatting away happily. Kia explained about her sister, Carrie, who she hadn't seen since the apocalypse started.

For the entire time of the apocalypse, she couldn't stop worrying about her sister's safety as she released all her feelings on to Caitlyn. Even though she hardly knew her, Caitlyn reminded Kia of her sister. She explained how Kai took her under his wing, rescuing her from a pack of zombies when she was left alone in her house.

"We'd better get back to our hideout," Kai said as he helped Scarlett off the floor, "Our families will start worrying."

Scarlett and Caitlyn could walk perfectly fine now as they felt their blood rush back to their bodies. Their friends were still feeling faint with their vision distorted as everyone helped them get to their feet, not wanting them to hurt themselves trying to get up alone.

They walked along the grass, making their way back to the road as they followed the signs to the beach. Jogging along the unmarked road; they huddled together in a group, keeping close till they arrived at the beach. They quietly ran down the pathway beside the glittering golden sand as they listened to the sea gently hitting the rigid rocks.

Daisy stopped in her steps as she took the breath-taking view in. She had imagined coming down here with her brother to have a picnic when he arrived back from the war but her plans had changed and so had the world. Seeing a sight like this was once in a life time experience now.

"Hurry up Daisy," Josh explained, seizing hold of her hand as he brought her back into reality.

Every shop they passed had been destroyed; items were missing, the doors had been pulled of their hinges and the windows had been smashed. The only thing that no one had touched was the cash machine as there was no point for money anymore. Anything anyone wanted, they just took or swapped with other survivors.

As they reached the end of the path; they turned sharply left, following a sign pointing towards a small forest which had relics of the bygone era scattered all over the grass. Cautiously, they stepped around them as they carried on walking.

Without warning, they suddenly paused as Kai listened to their surroundings. He sensed danger as he swiftly turned around, seeing a group of zombies hastily running towards them. They ran for their lives, dodging every tree in their way as they darted towards the road beside the spacious forest.

It didn't take them long to lose the zombies which had been lurking behind the trees as they carried on walking to their hideout. After a few minutes of walking beside a long brick wall, they finally arrived beside part of a wall that was covered in nettles and ivy.

Parts of the wall had crumbled away with age as the ivy darted in and out of small, unnoticeable gaps within the wall. Daisy and her friends didn't understand why they had stopped as they couldn't see any doors.

"This is our hideout," Kai explained.

"Stinging nettles and weeds?" Caitlyn said puzzled.

"It's a bunker," Kia laughed as she grabbed a long stick, pushing the weeds and nettles out of the way to reveal a long tunnel with a rusty metal door at the end.

Something seemed strange about the new hideout but none of them had much of a choice as they didn't have anywhere else to go. At least it was safer than being outside.

Scarlett looked down at the handle not wanting to touch it as she saw a cobweb dangling from it.

Kia pushed against the door as it swung open, showing a long dark tunnel which seemed to be endless. It was cold and smelt of dampness as they all shivered before continuing on their walk. Kia made sure she hid the entrance to the tunnel once again by putting the stinging nettles and weeds back over the entrance.

As they reached the end, they noticed a small old metal door standing in front of them. Kai knocked three times as he waited another few minute before knocking one more time.

They stood in silence as the door slowly creaked open. A man and a woman around the age of 30 stood in the door way, stopping them from entering the compound as Kai gestured them out of the way. They rushed inside, shutting the door behind them as Kia locked it.

Chapter 13
The Lab Plan

Daisy and her friends stood still in silence as they looked around the fairly average sized room which was full of strangers that were staring back at them with their beady little eyes. Once again they were feeling like outcasts and unwanted as the strangers folded their arms and scowled at them.

The room was dull and gloomy which seemed to express the sadness within the bunker walls. Moss was growing uncontrollably up the walls as they saw cobwebs dangle above them. Scarlett backed away slightly, once again showing her fear of spiders as she shivered with the thought of being near one.

The floor was uneven and made of broken stone like parts of the wall. Some of the walls had been vandalised, while other parts had graffiti covering it. Scarlett noticed some of the graffiti was meaningful whilst others she couldn't understand. There were a few parts that were clean and had no marks from anyone, but most of it was run down, showing the length of time it had been standing.

A middle aged lady elbowed her way through the crowd as she heard everyone whisper her son's name. She stopped, standing at the front of the crowd with her face lighting up as she saw him again. He had survived and that was the miracle she had hoped for.

The lady ran over to Kai and Kia with her arms outstretched ready to hug them. Her arms flung tightly round them both like a snake trapping its prey as she gave them a massive hug, showing how happy she was to be reunited with them.

"I was getting so worried about you two," the lady cried, shedding tears as she spoke.

"I told you not to worry. I promised you we would be safe," Kai answered, "I even brought Kia back safely like I said I would."

"That's my baby boy," the lady said, smiling as she patted him gently on the head.

"Careful of my hair, mum," Kai answered.

He gently began smoothing his hair out, trying to get it back to the style it was originally. His mum laughed while Kia giggled too as they watched him fiddle with his hair uncontrollably. He frowned at them both, sighing before he gave in.

The rest of the group that Kai had taken with him, had all ran off in the bunker to meet their families once again. Just like Kai, they were excited to see their parents and siblings if they had any as well as their friends. What they were looking forward most of all was a nice long nap after a long journey.

"Who are the newbie's?" a tall man rudely asked in a deep manly voice, interrupting Kai's reunion with his mum as he pointed at Daisy and her friends.

"That's... actually we didn't catch all of your names. What are your names?" Kai asked.

"I'm Scarlett, that's Daisy and her brother Josh, Emily, Cameron, Lewis, Abigail and her sister Jessica," Scarlett explained, pointing to each one of her friends as she said their names.

"And you are?" the tall man said as he turned to Caitlyn.

"I'm Caitlyn. Who are you?" she answered, giving him attitude.

"You don't need to know that information. You're not staying!" He replied.

Looking around, he saw everyone listening to him, hanging onto his every word. He wanted to be the leader so badly, instead of having to vote on everything all the time. Scarlett stared at him, knowing that he didn't want them there as she felt like an outcast once again.

"We don't have enough room as it is. Where are we supposed to put them!" the man continued to complain.

"We will find room for them. I'm not going to make them leave while we live in this type of world. I will not be responsible for their deaths," Kai shouted angrily.

Kia skipped over to Caitlyn as she gave her a humungous hug. Caitlyn froze in shock for a few seconds before awkwardly hugging her back. Kia didn't want Caitlyn and her friends to leave as they were the first nice people they had seen in a long time.

The two of them looked over at the tall man who was staring impatiently at Caitlyn and Kia. The unhappy man could see how much Caitlyn meant to her especially since she didn't know where her sister was. He knew she was starting to love her like a sister and he couldn't break them up.

"Fine, they can stay! Enjoy finding rooms for them all," the man answered, giving Kai a foul look.

"It will be fine. Will you stop worrying Robert," Kai answered.

Robert had always been the kind of person to feel better when he was left alone. He never liked being surrounded by people or crowds. In the bunker, he always kept his distance from everyone. Kai and his mum had tried to show him that there was more to the world than being alone but he didn't want to listen.

He walked over to his mum as he began thinking of a way to make everything work, after all he did get them this far, knowing they would be safe within the bunker walls. For all he knew they could be the last of humanity.

"If it helps; there are a few extra bunk beds in Kia's room as well as mine," Kai's mum explained.

"Perfect, everyone has a place to sleep," Kai said as he turned towards Robert who was standing in the door way, giving them a filthy look.

Robert grunted as he forced his way through the crowd, shoving everyone out of his way. The crowd quickly parted into two, letting him pass as none of them wanted to be pushed out of the way. None of them liked Robert very much due to his attitude towards everything, making him feel like he was alone in the world when he was surrounded by so many.

Daisy leant against the wall, chatting with her friends as they waited for someone to tell them what was happening. Kai walked over to where Daisy and her friends were standing as he pulled Caitlyn, Daisy, Scarlett, Josh and Lewis aside, leaving the other four friends to talk alone. The five of them looked at Kai worriedly.

"Okay, I'm going to get straight to the point. I know you want to end this apocalypse and I know how we can do that!" Kai explained, "I've been working on a plan for a few months now, I call it the operation lab plan."

"So what's the plan? How can we help?" Josh asked as his face lit up with the idea of the apocalypse finally ending.

"All I know is that it started in a hospital lab. I did a lot of research and running around till I found out the lab it all began with, which is only a few blocks away from here. All we have to do is get there without being noticed! I'm not exactly sure how to end it but hopefully when we get there, you'll come up with an idea," he explained.

"And how do you expect us to do that? It's probably crawling with zombies," Caitlyn asked as Kia walked over to them.

"I've seen you lot kill. I'm pretty sure you can handle this. Anyway you're a smart group, I'm sure you'll figure it out," Kai answered.

They were unaware of Kia who was listening to their conversation as she whistled casually. She started walking towards them as she tapped her foot impatiently, ready to interrupt them. Josh stared at her as she smirked before walking towards Caitlyn who looked at her. Kia stopped as she leaned against Caitlyn before folding her arms.

"What are you up to now?" Kia said, "You know your mum doesn't like it when you come up with plans."

"Go away Kia. This is a private conversation between me and them. It has nothing to do with you," Kai replied.

"Why can't I be part of it? I'm tough and you know it," Kia huffed as she began quivering her bottom lip to make it look like she was going to cry.

"It's too dangerous for you. You're just a kid," Josh explained.

"Kid... Kid! I'm a few years younger than you. If the lab plan isn't dangerous for you, then it's not dangerous for me either. Please let me join," Kia begged.

"Just leave please Kia," Kai answered.

"Well without me, you're not going anywhere. I have the plans and the map. So you can either take me or forget about the plan altogether," Kia explained.

Kia held the plans, which Kai had written on, in her petite hands as she waved it around in their faces trying to show off. They all stared at her in shock as they didn't realise how manipulative she could be. After all she was only a small 14-year-old girl but she had the attitude of a 17-year-old.

Again they saw what the apocalypse had done to the younger population. It hadn't just taken her childhood away; it had taken away her innocence. She would have never dared to talk back to anyone before but now it had become part of her survival to live.

Kai huffed as he thought he had hidden the plans away in a safe place, where he thought no one would look. He didn't understand how she got into his room and found it. Especially after he had put it in the best hiding place that he could think of.

"Don't be so shocked. Do you really think a pillow is the best hiding place for something like this?" Kia laughed as she gave them a massive cheeky grin, "Your mum lets me in there all the time to get a book to read."

"How did you find it though?" Josh asked.

"It wasn't even in the pillow properly," Kia replied.

"Fine you can come but be careful. I don't want to have to come back and say you're dead to my mum. I would never live it down," Kai said, "We leave in an hour!"

"You know you haven't explained the plan properly yet. So what is it and what do we need to do?" Scarlett asked.

"We're going to split up into four groups. Daisy and Lewis will be keeping the coast clear. Josh and I will be getting the guns and knives we need. Caitlyn and Kia will guard the map and wait with Scarlett and Jessica by the front door for us," Kai explained, "We'll meet you lot by the door in an hour!"

An hour went by as the group rushed to meet Caitlyn, Kia, Scarlett and Jessica by the bunker door. Everyone that was living in the bunker was busy having dinner as Kai threw a gun at Caitlyn and Josh. While Lewis gave Daisy and Scarlett a knife, giving them the handle first as he held the blades safely.

With the group prepared for the outside world again, Kai began unlocking all the locks on the door as he opened it. He hurriedly rushed them outside as he quickly shut it behind them. They entered the tunnel, running through the puddles as they arrived at the first door. Without a second thought the group opened it and lunged themselves out into the road in front.

They hastily ran around, ducking behind over filled bins that had spread across the floor, as well as overturned cars whenever they heard or saw any zombies. It wasn't that they were cowards; they just didn't want to die as this plan was too important.

None of them could risk getting caught right now as they needed to get to that lab before the zombies completely took over the world. Soon humans wouldn't be able to fight against the zombies as they would turn on their own kind for food and supplies, not caring about the outcome. They needed to stop it before it happened.

They walked through the town as they saw every house that they walked past had been broken into. Nearly every building looked as if they had been deserted. The town looked like a ghost town as if no one had ever lived there. It looked too dangerous for anyone to survive in now as it had become a playground for zombies.

Daisy looked at the houses as she noticed some of the doors had bloody lines from where the infected had once lived before they had completely turned into zombies. Most people had tried to keep themselves contained to stop the spreading of the virus but it didn't work. Now those people who had the virus making it was spread quicker.

Whilst walking around the group saw pieces of paper floating gently, fighting against the wind as it struggled to stay in one place. One piece blew into Scarlett's face as she pulled it off, beginning to read it out loud. There were hundreds of names listed on it with their ages and blood types but no photographs or names. In the top right hand corner of the paper, she noticed the name of the lab and its address.

"Lucinda's Hospital and Lab," Scarlett shouted, reading it off the paper, "It's minutes away. At the end of this road. We have to turn left, follow the road till you see a sign saying Lucinda Road, then turn right and it should be in front of you. That's not hard."

Chapter 14
Room 179

As soon as Scarlett had read the hospitals name, she knew exactly where to go as she had visited the town whilst growing up. Lucinda's Hospital was her birth place as well as her sisters. Her brothers had been born in a different hospital as her family didn't always live in the same place.

She zoned out thinking about the last day she had with her family and the argument which caused her to go for a drive. All she wanted was some peace and quiet which seemed impossible where she lived. Scarlett loved driving past the boarding school and adored its design, wishing she went there. She always wondered what would have happened if she was born into a different family. Would she have attended the school?

Since that first day of the apocalypse, she only found one good reason for her being there that day and that was knowing Daisy and her friends would have died if she didn't help them. If she hadn't gone for a drive, none of them would have made it. She still felt guilty about Ella, Zack and Amy but she knew their deaths weren't her fault as there wasn't anything she could have done to save them.

"Are you okay Scarlett?" Daisy asked as she looked at her worriedly.

"I'm fine," she replied, "Let's go."

After 5-10 minutes of running down straight roads and hiding from the zombies, they had finally reached their destination as they quickly turned around the last corner. A huge building stood in front of them, towering over the thousands of zombies below that had gathered in the parking lot, stopping everyone from entering.

Lewis and Kai rushed over to the dumpster and started hitting and kicking it in order to distract the zombies. The rest of the group ran as fast as they could, towards the building.

All of a sudden Kia fell over, skimming her knees against the ground causing them to bleed. The zombies twisted around, their bodies twitching as they walked towards Kia and the group. Caitlyn turned as she sprinted towards Kia grabbing her by the arm and pulling her up onto her feet. They bolted for the building holding tightly onto each other's hands.

The zombies were inches behind them, ready to seize their moment to attack as Kai picked up a large rock. He threw it hard at a zombie's head making it turn as its eyes were now staring at Lewis and Kai. Caitlyn and Kia carried on towards the building, slamming the door behind them. Daisy started stacking chairs against the door to block the entrance as her friends joined in. Within a couple of minutes, a few zombies arrived at the door, banging their fists against it.

Whilst Daisy and her friends where safe inside the building, Lewis and Kai had been left alone to fend for themselves against the zombies who had now cornered them by the dumpster. They looked worriedly at each other as they saw more zombies quickly gathering around them. Lewis opened the dumpster lid and instantly jumped inside without a second thought, slamming the lid shut on top of them.

They held the lid shut as the zombies started pounding it. The dumpster began shaking as fear flooded through their bodies. The boys screamed as the dumpster slowly started tipping over. Lewis and Kai fell onto their sides banging their hips as it fell. Kai opened the lid an inch before quickly pulling it shut again as a zombie's hand reached for them.

"What are we going to do?" Lewis whispered.

"I don't know," Kai answered.

"I'm going to die, aren't I? And It's your fault," Lewis said angrily.

"My fault! How? You could have stayed behind but you didn't!" Kai shouted, "I never pressured you into doing this. You chose to, so don't you dare blame me."

Without warning, a skinny hand slowly lifted the lid. Kai quickly grabbed an empty bottle which lay next to him as he smashed it against the hand, letting glass shatter everywhere. Suddenly, the lid slammed shut almost catching Kai's hand in the process.

"Ow," a voice said in pain as the lid began opening once again.

The lid flung back, making a loud thud as it hit the back of the bin. Scarlett stood in front of them holding her bloody hand which was covered in small shards of glass. Kai and Lewis blushed with embarrassment as they both crawled out of the dumpster. The two boys brushed the rubbish off themselves as they looked at Scarlett's hand.

"I'm so sorry Scarlett," Kai explained, "If I knew it was you, I wouldn't have done it. You know that right?"

"Of course I do but I was coming to help you. Even though I'm starting to think it might have been a mistake!" Scarlett said as she looked down at her hand which was now throbbing with pain.

"Sorry, we thought you were a zombie," Lewis explained.

"Really? Do I look dead? Don't even answer that!" Scarlett said unimpressed.

Kai looked at Scarlett who was carefully picking the splinters of glass out of her hand. He felt so guilty that he had caused her pain when she didn't deserve it. He ripped part of his sleeve off as he started to wrap it around Scarlett's hand. She smiled as he bandaged her hand up tightly as he tried to stop the blood flow.

"We'd better get back to the rest," Lewis explained, "We don't want them to worry. Do we?"

Lewis, Scarlett and Kai darted towards the building, heading for the front door as they weaved in and out through the zombie crowd. A few zombies turned their heads as they slowly walked after them. None of them looked back as they kept their eyes on the door.

They saw everyone rush to the doors as Daisy and the group began moving all of the chairs that had blocked the entrance. Daisy swiftly opened the door as her three friends entered. Instantly she slammed the door shut after them as they began stacking the chairs back against the door, shoving a few under the handles so they couldn't budge.

"Now what?" Josh asked, "Where's the lab?"

"On the third floor, room 179," Kai explained, "I don't know the way to it though."

"You dragged us all here but you don't know how to get to room 179," Josh replied.

"Well to be honest, I didn't think you'd actually go through with my plan, let alone get here alive," Kai answered truthfully.

They turned their heads as they looked around, taking every detail in. The walls had been freshly painted white with a blue and pink stripe through the middle as wet paint signs were pinned up to warn them. A map hung on the wall which was partly ripped, showing each room in the entire building including the fire exits.

Blood was dripping from the ceiling, leaving stains on the beige tiled flooring. There was a white staircase to the left of them, leading to the first floor. Kia ran up them without thinking, to check if the coast was clear as Caitlyn chased after her. Josh and Kai walked over to the wall which held the map, trying to find the room they needed. While Scarlett, Lewis and Daisy watched out for any zombies, holding tightly onto their guns.

"Found it," Kai said as he pointed at the map, "Walk up two flights of stairs and turn left. Follow the corridor till you see a sign saying 3 and then turn right. Room 179 should be along that corridor."

Without a second thought, they followed the directions that Kai had given them. Every corridor they ran past looked exactly the same as the last. All of the corridors were quiet and plain but as they entered the last one, everything changed.

There was a crowd of zombies, waiting for them as they froze in their steps. All of the zombies were wearing long white lab coats with ID cards pinned onto them, showing glimpses of their old identities. Caitlyn was last to enter the zombie infested corridor. She saw her friend's reaction and grabbed her gun from her pocket, getting ready to shoot.

A rotten hand seized hold of her gun as if the zombie was trying to wrestle with her over it. Caitlyn wasn't going to let go of her gun that easily as she shoved the gun into its mouth, pointing towards its brain before pulling the trigger, letting it drop down dead.

As Daisy turned around, she saw Scarlett pinned up against the wall by a zombie. Her gun was lying on the other side of the corridor, leaving Scarlett helpless as another zombie approached her. Daisy grabbed her knife, stabbing the zombie in its back without hesitation as its teeth dug into Scarlett's arm.

She screamed in agony. Her skin hung off as blood oozed out, dripping onto the cold stone floor. Its teeth gradually dug further into her arm, ripping at her flesh as Daisy stabbed the zombie in its brain several times, splitting its head in two. Scarlett dropped to the floor as she shivered and twitched uncontrollably.

"She's going to turn into one of them!" Josh explained, pulling Daisy away from Scarlett, for her own safety.

"We can't leave her here! There's still time to save her, we can't give up," Kai said.

Josh ran over to Scarlett's gun; seizing hold it before pointing the gun at the zombies. He pulled the trigger as one by one they dropped down dead in front of him. The gunshot echoed throughout the hallway as they froze, hearing a loud bang. Lewis and Caitlyn picked Scarlett up, lifting her carefully into their arms as they carried on walking down the corridor. Caitlyn kept an eye on Kia as Kai led the way to room 179.

Daisy looked over at Scarlett with tears in her eyes. Goosebumps shivered down her body as she tried not to cry. Her stomach twisted and turned, making her feel sick as she bit the inside of her lip nervously. Scarlett had become one of their closest friends and Daisy didn't want to lose another friendship. She knew if the virus remained; they would all end up alone, it didn't matter if they were dead or alive. It would end the same way for them all.

As they walked further down the corridor, a shadow swiftly drifted past them. Daisy gripped her gun tightly, still trying to control her feelings as she slowly moved ahead of her friends. All of a sudden a man grabbed her, dragging her away into room 179 as he put his hand over her mouth to stop her screaming.

"Mr Peters is that you?" Daisy asked in a muffled voice, "Why are you here, in room 179?"

Daisy recognised him as she would often see him with Ella, as he was her father. Ella hardly ever saw him as he spent most all of his time, face down in his work. He wouldn't tell any of his three children; Ella, Claire and Jeremy about his work as he always said it was private.

"Yes Daisy. Now what are you doing here," Mr Peters replied, slowly releasing her.

"What do you think? We're looking for a cure!" she explained.

Daisy ran out of the room as she heard another crash. Scarlett was seizing on the floor covered in blood as her body tensed up. Her eyes began glowing red as she arched her back painfully. Mr Peters pushed Daisy out the way as he grabbed hold of Scarlett before tying her to a chair with rope.

"I can't do this anymore, it's too painful," Scarlett cried, screaming as she clenched her fists, slamming her back against the chair.

Droplets of sweat slowly dripped down her forehead as she breathed heavily, coughing up blood. Her heart started beating faster as her body began seizing again. Her body trembled as she shook her head viciously, gasping for air. Kai looked at her worriedly. He put his hand gently on her shoulder as she passed out, letting her head drop to the side. His eyes widened at the thought of her being a zombie.

Without warning, she snapped at him, trying to bite his hand. She was a zombie. Guilt spread across Mr Peters face as he held a photo of his three children in his hands. He gulped, staring silently at Scarlett who was thrashing around angrily out of control. She growled at everyone as her jaw snapped open and shut continuously. The more she tried to bite them, the angrier she got.

"I haven't been entirely truthful with all of you," Mr Peters explained, "I started this apocalypse. It was an accident. I didn't mean to hurt anyone."

"But you did," Lewis replied slowly, his eyebrows were arched as he stopped talking, leaving his mouth wide open in shock.

"Most of the world is gone!" Josh answered, "including people you once loved."

"You're the reason that Ella, Zack and Amy are dead! So many people are dead because of you," Daisy shouted.

"Ella's dead!" Mr Peters said in shock, "What have I done, it's my fault."

There was an awkward pause as everyone felt the pain Mr Peters was going through. He didn't know what he had done to his daughter, cutting her life short because of an accident he had caused. If he had left the lab and worked as a teacher like Ella's aunt did, she might have lived longer than she did. It was too late now; he couldn't bring her back, no one could.

"So… How did it start?" Kai asked, as he kept looking over at Scarlett.

Chapter 15
Bite of Death

"It started a month ago. My co-workers were trying to find a cure while I worked on a secret project the government had given me. One of my co-workers knocked a test tube of mine over, spilling it on his body as well as my desk. He went to clean it up but that's where it all started. As soon as he touched his skin to wipe it off, it started pealing as if he was badly sunburnt. Then his pupils changed colour, they were a disgusting shade of green to start with but then it turned to a dark red. Finally, his behaviour changed, becoming aggressive as he started killing everyone in his way. He was a monster," Mr Peters explained, "It took a lot of bullets and people to stop him but unfortunately by the time we had killed him, the virus had contaminated everyone he had touched."

"Maybe it's not too late to fix everything," Lewis said, "if you made this virus, you can end it. Right?"

"I've been trying to create a cure since it started but it's harder than it looks. It takes the right equipment and chemicals as well as the right amount of time, which we seem to be running out of," Mr Peters interrupted. "The closest I've ever got to turning one back was for an hour that's it."

"Well that's better than nothing. Why don't you give that to Scarlet? I can't stand to see her like this," Daisy asked.

"Because of the side affect's," he said, "If you think the apocalypse is bad right now, then imagine this. Their hearing, sight and sense of smell a thousand times better than before. They could find us from a mile away without even seeing or hearing us. They can sense us by using the vibrations in the ground. We would be dead instantly! We'd be hunted alive. There would be nowhere to hide!"

All of a sudden Scarlett took a long gasp of air as she stopped moving. She stared into space, not blinking as her eyes slowly closed. Everyone looked in her direction. Josh cautiously leant over her still body, opening her eyes carefully with his fingers as he saw her eyes had changed. They weren't red anymore; they had now turned an ocean blue colour with dark red spots floating around.

Her skin turned back to its normal colour, making her look like herself again. No longer did she look infected. There was still blood on her top from when she had turned into a zombie but now she was had turned into a human again. She wasn't a zombie or was she?

"What's happened? Why am I tied up?" Scarlett asked, looking around confused.

"You're not a zombie anymore. You're cured," Kai said happily.

"I'm sorry," Kia said, "I didn't listen to hear about the side effects."

Kia stood by the front door holding a needle in her hand as everyone looked her way. She dropped it. As it fell it smashed, letting shards of glass dance across the floor. She was never the type of person to listen to an entire conversation. Normally she would take parts of it and act upon what she had heard. This time she knew she had messed up as the look on their faces told her that the cure wasn't ready, it wasn't safe.

"What have you done?" Mr Peters shouted at Kia.

"Don't shout at her, she's just a kid!" Caitlyn said, standing up for Kia.

"I'm not a kid," Kia said under her breath as she folded her arms.

"She's doomed us all!" Mr Peters said angrily, "We might as well give up now!"

"That's your attitude to everything, isn't it?" Caitlyn replied.

"Wait! What's happening? Can someone tell me what I've missed? I feel like I've been hit on the head with a baseball bat," Scarlett said, even more confused than before.

"Long story short; you were bit and turned. Kia stupidly injected you with the false cure and soon you'll be a zombie, deadlier than before wanting to kill everything in your path," Josh explained.

Noise rustled in the corridor as everyone stopped speaking, freezing in their tracks. They ducked behind the desks, leaving Scarlett tied to the chair in the view of anything that walked past the door. Scarlett gradually slipped down the chair trying to make herself less visible. A zombie moaned as it walked past the door dragging one of it leg's behind.

"Is it gone?" Scarlett whispered.

"I don't know," Daisy answered, "I'll have a look."

Daisy stood up as she carefully walked over to the door, taking each step with extra care. She couldn't see anything as she peered through the glass in the door, staring out into the hallway. Slowly she turned her back around to face her friends, seeing no threat outside the room.

The glass shattered as a gruesome hand suddenly shot through it, grabbing her tightly by her neck. She screamed as its grip got tighter. Raising her arms, she tried to peel the zombie's hands off her neck covering her own hands in blood. She screamed once more as she began gasping for air.

"Help me," she said, beginning to choke.

"Daisy!" Josh shouted as he rushed over to help his beloved sister.

Within seconds the zombie had smashed its head through the window still grasping tightly onto Daisy. She couldn't turn around as her body was glued to the door by the zombie's grip. It leaned its head further into the room, reaching for Daisy's neck. Its jaw clicked as it opened its mouth ready to take a bite out of her.

Daisy closed her eyes as she tried her hardest to block out the pain from the zombie. It launched its mouth at her pale neck, piercing through her skin as blood dripped down. She shivered as her eyes widened. They could see the pain within her eyes as she squinted through the agony, almost in tears.

Josh ran towards her. He seized hold of the zombie's bloody arm, pushing it against the door making it snap as it let go of Daisy. She dropped to the floor gasping for air as Josh bent down beside her. A tear dripped down her face as she covered part of her neck with her hand as Josh hadn't realised she was bitten.

He lifted her hand, noticing the bite mark as he moved her hair out of the way, trying to comfort her as much as possible. His skin turned cold as he started sniffling before bursting into tears. She was all he had and now he was losing her too. He was going to be alone in the world without any family to keep close.

He sat her up against the wall as her head rocked back and forth. She felt too weak as she lost control over her body. Her head dropped to one side, letting her eyes gently close as she felt a bright light call her deeper into the darkness of her soul.

Everyone stared at her in shock. Kai wrapped his arms around Kia as Caitlyn and Lewis joined the group hug, trying to comfort each other. Mr Peters picked up her floppy body as he tied her to a chair like Scarlett. Josh stared at his beloved sister, he didn't want to let her go but he had no choice. Soon she would be just another zombie wanting to eat them.

"I love you my sister. I will always remember you, I could never forget you," Josh said holding her hands with his head on her lap as he cried.

"I'm not gone yet," Daisy whispered as she pushed through the pain, "I won't leave you, not yet!"

"We need that cure and now," Lewis explained.

"We only have 45minutes left till Scarlett will be unstoppable and it will be the end of the world," Kai said.

"Let's get to work then. Do you lot want to be my lab partners?" Mr Peters asked.

"Sure," they answered in unison.

"Lewis please get me the purple and green bottle from the cupboard. Caitlyn get the syringe and the needles from the white plastic box on my desk. Kai get the glass tubes on the corner table," Mr Peters ordered them.

Lewis rushed to the cupboard as he pulled the door wide open. A man in a white lab coat lay dead on the floor. He had no bite marks or scratches; there was just blood and bullet hole. His left arm looked sore as it was covered in bloody red spots, almost looking like chicken pox but worse. It looked as if his skin had been burnt as half of his skin was covered in red boils. A gun lay beside the man's dead body surrounded by bullets.

"Who is this man?" Lewis asked.

"He was the person that spilled the chemicals at the beginning, he's also the first person to turn," Mr Peters said, "He was a good friend and a great co-worker."

"What happened to him? Why does his body have so many bullet holes in?" Lewis asked.

"Unfortunately, we had to shoot him. He left us with no choice, he was attacking everyone. The virus attached itself to him as it started spreading quickly. The people who got infected went home to their families, not knowing that they were carriers of the virus. After that it got out of our hands, that's when the virus really began," Mr Peters explained.

Lewis was speechless as he walked into the cupboard. He carefully stepped around the body, making sure he didn't touch it as he didn't know if the virus was still living within his body. As he took his last step over the figure, he felt something cold grab his leg. Lewis looked down as he saw the dead man's arm attached to him.

He looked at him in shock as he tried to pull his leg free. With the amount of bullet holes in the man's body, Lewis thought he would definitely be dead. No one not even a zombie could survive that many bullets. The man suddenly sat up straight, staring into space as he still held onto Lewis's leg, making him scream.

"Grab the gun," Mr Peters shouted, "and shoot him!"

Lewis did as he was told as he reached for the gun. He couldn't reach it with the dead guy still holding onto him. As he lifted his knee up, knocking into the zombie's jaw as it fell backwards, letting go of Lewis. Swiftly he grabbed the gun as he fell onto the floor. He turned around as he faced the zombie.

Lewis shot the monster twice in the head as he tried to aim for his skull before shooting him one last time, making sure he was dead. The zombie dropped dead for the final time as Lewis reached for the two bottles before hastily running out of the cupboard, slamming the door shut. He quickly locked the cupboard door for safety. Even though he had shot the zombie in its head, he still didn't know whether it was dead for sure.

"You could have warned me!" Lewis shouted.

"If I had told you he was there; would you have gone in? Anyway I thought he was dead," Mr Peters explained, taking the bottles from Lewis as he put them on his work surface.

Kai had already got the glass tubes and watched as Mr Peters set them out in a certain order on the table. Meanwhile Caitlyn searched for the syringe and needles in the box. Within a few minutes she rushed over, putting them next to the glass tubes before walking over to Kia. Caitlyn felt as if Kia had become like a sister to her in the short time that she knew her, feeling as if it was her job to protect Kia from anything the world threw at her.

Mr Peters mixed the liquids inside the purple bottle before tipping it into the green one. He shook the liquids as everyone watched. Without a care in the world, he pricked his finger letting a drop of blood fall into the mixture. Finally, he added a pinch of salt and a few random ingredients before mixing them altogether.

He picked up the syringe as he measured it, taking the samples as he let it enter the tubes of the needles. Carefully he walked over to Scarlett and Daisy who sat twitching uncomfortable on their chairs. Daisy and Scarlett looked at the needles, fear grew in their eyes.

"Who wants to test it first?" Mr Peters asked.

Daisy shook her head ferociously as Scarlett stared at her. Neither of them liked needles as they both hated the idea of something piercing their skin. Daisy didn't want to be the first to try it as she didn't know what it would do. Scarlett looked at Mr Peters and nodded as she decided to try the cure first instead.

"I will," Scarlett said as she gave a little smile to Daisy.

"Okay," Mr Peters replied.

Mr Peters gently pierced Scarlett's skin as he put the needle into her arm, injecting the serum slowly into her system. She flinched as a shooting pain ran through her veins and down her legs. Everyone stared at Scarlett waiting for the outcome to happen.

"What do we do now?" Kai asked.

"We just have to wait and see!" Mr Peters answered.

"How long will it take," Josh asked, impatiently.

"I don't know, this is the first time I've tried this serum," Mr Peters explained.

Chapter 16
Take a Chance

They waited and waited as they watched Scarlett like a hawk; waiting for her to show a reaction to the first sample of the cure she had been given. No one knew how deadly the serum was nor did they know if it would work. It was a risk they had to take for the sake of humanity. Mr Peters went back to his desk as he gently rested his head upon it whilst waiting.

As five minutes passed by, Scarlett began shaking viciously as sweat poured down her forehead. Her eyes turned a light orange as the lights above her flickered slightly. Lewis touched her head as he felt the heat rush to his hands. A throbbing pain rushed through her head as she moaned in agony.

As she tried to move her foot, pins and needles shot through her body. Her throat felt dry as her body felt as if it was being weighed down, pinning her to the floor. With no energy, her body slumped against the back of the chair. Mr Peters had given Scarlett a fever that was draining all of her energy from her body.

Scarlett looked miserable and depressed as every pair of eyes were glued to her, making her feel uncomfortable. Daisy stared at her, trying to move her chair further away from Scarlett and Mr Peters as she knew that it would soon be her time to face her fear of needles.

"I feel so weak, everywhere hurts," Scarlett moaned, "What have you done to me!"

Mr Peters watched Scarlett's every movement, paying extra close attention to everything she did as he needed to make sure he had every precise detail noted. He listed the ingredients in order of what he had used for the first cure, into his leather note book.

"Cure 1, side effects: sweating, change of eye colour to light orange, fever, pains, pins and needles, dry throat, lethargic and aching," Mr Peters said as he wrote it down, "Not a usable cure at all!"

Scarlett's fever finally started to calm down as she looked at everybody with her eyes which were once again an amazing ocean blue colour which suited her hair perfectly. Mr Peters had begun making the second serum, carefully stirring each ingredient into the liquid. It started bubbling as a cloud of smoke raised into the air, before disappearing into its surroundings.

Mr Peters looked at it uncertainly as he tipped it into the tubes for Daisy who was looking worriedly at her blood thirsty friend next to her. Scarlett stared at Daisy with hunger in her eyes, dribble slipped down her chin as her mouth hung open. The 1st serum that Mr Peters had given Scarlett had stopped the side effects from the dose Kia had given her by mistake but it didn't stop her from turning back.

Scarlett had now turned into a normal zombie once again as her stunning blue eyes disappeared in a cloud of red blood that surrounded them. Slowly her skin started peeling from her chin as blood started covering her body. Daisy yelled as she struggled to untie the rope that held her to the seat.

Josh hastily gripped Daisy's chair, dragging her away from Scarlett to keep her from being bitten again. He knelt beside her with tears still in his eyes as he held his younger sister's hand. Mr Peters quickly put the 2nd serum into a clean new needle as he walked over to Daisy, trying to keep away from Scarlett's grasp.

He tapped the end of the needle, a few droplets leaked out as he took her arm carefully. Her face turned pale as she squirmed at the sight of the needle. She looked away as he injected it into her arm. Within seconds she started screaming for water as she grabbed her neck. Her sharp nails scratching away at her skin as hundreds of cuts suddenly appeared.

"I need water," She screamed as Josh ran over to his bag, grabbing a bottle of water.

He handed the bottle over to Daisy as she seized hold of it before unscrewing the lid and tipping it into her mouth. Daisy gulped the cool water down, making sure she didn't waste a single droplet. Even with the bottle she had just drunk, she still could feel her dry throat aching for more water.

"Not enough," She yelled, "I need more water. NOW!"

"Calm down Daisy," Caitlyn spoke softly.

"I can't! I feel irritated at everything you lot do," Daisy explained, "Please help us!"

"She'll be fine," Mr Peters shouted as everyone fell silent.

With one last moan, she released the grip on her neck, leaving red hand prints implanted on it as she thrusted her hand at her heart. She could feel the racing pulse as she began yawning, feeling exhausted. Her eyes slowly began to shut as she drifted in and out of consciousness. Wrinkles appeared under her eyes as they fully closed.

It didn't take Daisy long to fall asleep as her head dropped forwards, making it look like she was dead. Josh watched Daisy's stomach as he made sure she was still breathing. She took a long breath in as Josh sighed with relief, still holding her hand tightly. Her breathing was getting shallower as he released his grip, taking a few steps back.

"Cure 2: Excessive thirst, scratching, dry throat, mood swings, pulse and heart racing, exhaustion and drowsiness," Mr Peters wrote in his book, "Again not a usable cure!"

"Why isn't this working? We're running out of time," Lewis asked as he complained, "We need it to work!"

A cluster of zombies suddenly thrashed angrily at the door as an arm burst through the broken window in the door, followed by hundreds more. The zombie group were wrestling each other to get through the small gap within the door as they stretched their arms through it. Pieces of shattered glass scratched their arms as they showed no signs of pain.

Everyone cried in panic as they let out loads of terrifying screams which echoed through the room. Mr Peters rushed to his desk as he started working on the 3rd cure. Quickly he seized hold of every item that he needed, mixing them cautiously together. The zombies were moaning loudly as they pushed their body weight against the door, trying to enter the room

"Keep them out. I need to make this cure!" Mr Peters said, "I can't have distractions."

"How are we supposed to do that?" Kia asked.

"There's a gun in the cupboard and two knives in a draw in the front desk," Mr Peters explained, "Don't ask why, just get them!"

"We have guns but we only have a few bullets left," Kai said, "Do you have any extra bullets?"

"The gun in the cupboard is fully loaded, you don't need your guns," he replied, "Stop talking and hurry up! We're running out of time."

Lewis and Kai looked at each other before rushing over to the desk as if they were having a race to grab the knives. Neither of them wanted to open the cupboard door, especially after last time. They opened the draws and began searching for the knives as all the paperwork within fell out, scattering onto the floor.

Caitlyn and Josh sprinted towards the cupboard, with no care in the world as Caitlyn flew the door open, releasing the smell from within. Both of them were shocked as they looked down upon the gun shot body lying on the bloody ground. Josh stared at Caitlyn as she began walking into the cupboard. He seized hold of her hand pulling her back as he shook his head.

"Are you sure it's definitely dead this time?" Josh asked as he glared at the body while Caitlyn quietly snuck in.

"It better be!" Lewis shouted to Josh, "It has been shot more than ten times."

Caitlyn quickly grabbed the gun before running out, almost falling into Josh who caught hold of her as he locked the door behind her. They leant against the door for a few minutes before running over to their friends who were already prepared to fight the zombies.

Meanwhile more zombies had arrived outside the room. Kai and Lewis stood with their backs against the wall beside the door, stabbing viciously at the zombie's hands and arms that flung through the broken window, where the glass once was. They held the knives tightly within their sweaty hands as they carried on protecting the room.

"I hope this works, for everyone's sake," Mr Peters said as he walked past Daisy and over to Scarlett.

Daisy's eyes were bloodshot as an evil grin spread widely across her face, showing her rotten teeth. She had awful breath which stank like rotten eggs and smelt like gas being released every time she took a breath. A stare of death came from her tired eyes, sending a cold dead vibe through anyone who looked at her.

She had now fully turned into a zombie, snarling at Mr Peters as he strode past her. Josh and Caitlyn were busy with Kai and Lewis trying to keep the zombies out of the room as they fought back. They were outnumbered by the zombies as Caitlyn seized hold of the gun.

"Stand back," Caitlyn shouted, "Kia stay out the way, I don't want you to get hurt!"

She raised the gun as she pointed it through the window, aiming for the zombie's heads. With each pull of the trigger, the gun shook as the bullets twisted through the air before crashing into their heads. There weren't enough bullets to kill all of them as more kept approaching, making it more difficult to protect everyone within the room.

Kia was in the far corner, trying to stay as far away from the door and the zombies as she could. Doing what Caitlyn had told her, she watched from a distance as she saw her friends defending the room and the cure which was being made inside.

Mr Peters stood next to Scarlett as he took hold of her scrawny arm which was enclosed in blood covered spots that stood out against her pale skin. Her eyes where a light red colour covered by her long hair that hung over her face.

He carefully put the needle that held a small trial amount into Scarlett's delicate arm, letting the serum flood through her veins and into her system as he waited for the results of the last trial. Scarlett started sweating as she closed her eyes in discomfort, trying to block out the noises which surrounded her.

Suddenly her body jumped as her eyes opened, showing her normal eye colour that rushed back to fight against the disease. Slowly the colour returned to her skin, making her look like a human once more. She looked completely normal, like nothing had ever happened to her.

"IT WORKED!" Mr Peters shouted with joy, "It worked, it really worked!"

"Finally!" Lewis shouted from the door.

"Well done, we knew you could do it," Josh replied, "Now save my sister for goodness sake."

"Okay, okay! Give me a minute!" Mr Peters answered.

He dawdled over to his desk as he took out a fresh needle, filling it with the serum before running over to Daisy. She snarled viciously at him, showing her painfully raw gums as she twisted her head towards him. With every snap of her reddened jaw, he fidgeted uncomfortable as he thought of a way to get the cure to her without being bitten.

"I need some help over here!" Mr Peters shouted, "Josh help me!"

"I'm coming," he replied.

Josh galloped towards them as he froze, shocked to see his sister a flesh eating zombie. She looked at Josh deeply in his eyes as if she remembered him before thrashing her body viciously in the chair but he knew she didn't. The virus wiped their memories, stopping them from acting like humans and turning them into hunters that pounced on any fresh meat they saw.

"Hold her down! Josh... Josh," Mr Peters shouted as they stood close to Daisy.

Josh slowly walked forwards, towards her as he put his hands carefully on either side of her head to keep it still. This was the only way he could think of that wouldn't hurt Daisy but would always keep her from biting Mr Peters.

The look in Daisy's eyes filled Josh with sadness as he stared at her face whilst Mr Peters prepared the needle for Daisy's arm. He picked up her arm, letting the needle pierce through her skin as the cure entered her blood stream.

She scrunched her eyes tightly as she gritted her teeth, showing the pain that she was in. Her head swung backwards, hitting the back of the chair as Josh fell back in shock. Blood slowly dripped down her neck as a small cut appeared on the back of her head. She started shivering uncontrollably as her skin grew paler and her breath grew shorter.

Within a few minutes her eyes had completely changed back to normal along with her skin. She yawned as she tried to cover her mouth, realizing that she was still tied to the chair. Daisy looked up at her brother who was staring back at her with lots of different emotions spreading across his face.

Chapter 17
The Injections

"You're cured!" Josh explained as he jumped for joy, wrapping his arms around her.

"Does that mean you can untie me now? It's not as comfortable as it might look" Daisy stated, looking down at the rope.

Josh instantly wrestled against the wrath of the rope as he struggled to untie Daisy. Meanwhile Mr Peters tried to give the correct dosage of the cure to Scarlett as she fidgeted restlessly, trying to fight against him. It was as if the zombie version of Scarlett knew what was in the needle and didn't want to turn back.

Daisy stood up, throwing the ropes onto the ground as she carefully walked towards Scarlett. She kneeled in front of Scarlett as she started waving her hands around; to distract her. Mr Peters inserted the needle carefully into her arm.

Just like Daisy, the cure instantly started to change Scarlett but not in the same way. Froth appeared around her mouth as she choked on her own breath. Her eyes closed as her entire body began to shake viciously. Mr Peters seized hold of a light, shining it in her eyes, he saw red blots spreading rapidly in the left eye.

"I don't know if the cure is working! It's acting differently to her body and I don't know why," Mr Peters explained.

"It'd better work, we can't lose her," Lewis shouted.

"I'm trying my hardest here!" he answered.

"I know," Lewis said under his breath, "That's what I'm afraid off!"

"I heard that!" Mr Peters shouted angrily.

"Whatever!" Lewis replied.

"Will you both just stop bickering for one moment and focus on the cure and Scarlett," Caitlyn spoke.

Lewis glanced at Mr Peters one last time before looking away as he returned back to the door, still trying to keep the zombies out with Caitlyn's help. Meanwhile Mr Peters carried on observing Scarlett who had still not changed back into a human.

All of a sudden her breath became shallower as she stopped breathing. She sat frozen on the chair as Mr Peters quickly loosened the rope, lying her on the floor. The rope was still tightened securely around her as she lay on her back, not moving. He looked at her worriedly as Lewis barged him out of his way.

He leaned over her placing one hand over the other as he began the compressions on the middle of her chest. With his heart beating fast and sweat falling down his forehead, he knew he couldn't give up hope. Scarlett needed him now more than ever and he needed to save her.

"Come on breath! You have to live Scarlett! Don't give up, come back to us," Lewis shouted as he continued the compressions.

"I think she's gone," Daisy said putting her hand on his shoulder.

"No she's not. She's still alive. I know she is," Lewis replied as tears fell from his face, "please Scarlett wake up!"

Daisy knelt beside him as she placed one arm around his shoulder, pulling him into a hug as she whispered, "It'll be okay Lewis."

With those words, Daisy stood up and she walked towards her brother who was looking past her in shock. She turned around as she saw Scarlett struggling to sit up as the rope forced her to stay lying down. The red blots that had once filled her left eye were gone.

Colour slowly returned to her skin as she looked up at everyone curiously. She didn't have the urge to bite anyone anymore. Her body had stopped trembling and sweating, showing she was back to her normal self.

Lewis could feel the joy rush through his body as he gave her a hug without thinking of how she would feel about it. Scarlett rolled her eyes but didn't try to push him away, knowing how much her friendship meant to him.

With all their friends once again human, Josh ran to Mr Peters desk to fill more needles with the cure. Kia watched him with her eyes wide open, observing his every move, fascinated with the idea of there being a cure at last. The human population could finally rest knowing that everyone could survive this disaster.

"Now untie me" Scarlett said as she raised her left eyebrow, "Thanks!"

"You're welcome," Mr Peters replied sarcastically, "you could at least say thank you without the sarcasm, maybe even once to show your appreciation of my hard work to create the cure to save you and your friends."

"I see we don't have much time," Scarlett answered as she looked over at the door which was slowly breaking.

Once that door breaks the zombies would fly in, dooming them to a life of eating human flesh. Unfortunately, with the cure in their systems, Daisy and Scarlett would die a horrible fate and wouldn't turn like their beloved friends and family. Instead they would live through the pain of being ripped apart and eaten alive.

A loud crash from the hallway caught Kia's attention as she moved away from the desk. She anxiously tiptoed towards the door as she peered through the window. Something didn't feel right as she couldn't see any of the zombies waiting to attack her and her friends.

What she didn't know was that all the zombies were still in the hallway but they were all knelt on the floor with their backs against the wall, trying to stay out of sight, having evolved without realising. All of a sudden the hoard of zombies pounced up from the ground, seizing hold of her by her arm.

"Help," Kia screamed.

"We need that cure over here now!" Kai shouted, running over to Kia who was squirming to get free.

Kai saw the fear in her eyes as he grabbed the zombies hand firmly, yanking it off of Kia's arm. Another gruesome hand barged its way through the shattered window seizing hold of Kia by her hair as she let out a terrifying shriek. Her whole head went numb from the pain as she held onto the zombie's hand, trying to stop it from pulling her hair any more than it already had.

"Be careful, we can't hurt them," Lewis shouted as he ran over to help.

"We know!" Kai answered, pulling Kia free with all of his strength.

They knew that they couldn't severely hurt the zombies as they couldn't bring them back if they were fully dead. At the moment their brains were still functioning as well as their bodies, even if they weren't acting like humans. They had just made the cure to save everyone but still had some questions left unsolved like how far the cure would spread and would it be the full time solution to the apocalypse.

It was up to them to save everyone in the world as they were the only ones who could save the world from total destruction. They were the only group of people who had been successful in creating the cure as far as they were aware, but somehow they knew that their fight to save humanity would not be over so quickly.

Josh grabbed a black bag that was left on the floor near Mr Peters desk and began filling it with needles that carried the cure before rushing over to the door to help his friends. Without a second thought everyone else gathered around the door which was blocked by the zombies.

"What are we going to do? We can't get out!" Kai asked, "We're trapped."

Mr Peters looked around the room, searching for another way out, before looking over to a small vent on the wall to his left. It was very close to the ceiling and he knew they wouldn't be able to reach it because none of them were tall enough. He grabbed a stool and ran towards it, putting it down beside the wall as he clambered on top.

"I have an idea! Someone can go through the vent and get into a different room. Then they can distract the zombies while we sneak up on them to give them the cure," Mr Peters explained.

Instantly the group looked over at Kia and then at Lewis and Daisy, knowing that they were the smallest in their group and perfect for the task. Caitlyn wasn't keen on the idea, looking worriedly at Kia, running over giving her a hug. She didn't want to let her go but knew that she had to, for the sake of humanity.

The two of them had started acting more like sisters since the first day that they had met, especially as Kia still didn't have any clue about the whereabouts of her own sister. It seemed like Kia wanted someone to take the place of her till she returned, which Caitlyn was more than happy to do. Caitlyn was an only child and had always wanted a younger sister or brother.

"You'll be okay, remember you're not a child anymore. You're strong, stronger than you think," Caitlyn said as Kia hugged her back.

Kia nodded as the three of them and Mr Peters lifted the vent hatch off. Mr Peters cupped his hands, letting Lewis put his foot on them, lifting him into the vents. Daisy went second as she put her foot into Mr Peters hands, giving her hand to Lewis, letting him pull her up in to the dusty air vents. Lastly it was Kia's turn as Daisy and Lewis reached their hands out to her, pulling her into the vents with them.

They scuttled around in the air vents which seemed to last forever, pushing cobwebs out of their way as they got covered in dust. There was a foul smell wafting through the air, reminding them of the dead people roaming within the building. A faint light shone at the end of the small vent as they hurried towards it, wanting to escape the endless maze of tunnels.

Without warning the vent collapsed, letting them fall into a room which seemed not to be too far away from the room 179 as they could still hear the hoard of zombies moaning. The room that they had dropped into seemed small and empty, with little furniture. One chair caught their eyes as it stood alone in the middle of the room covered in blood and broken glass.

"Is everyone okay?" Daisy asked.

"Yes," Kia replied.

The three of them gathered their strength as they quickly stood up. Lewis ran to the door, ignoring Kia and Daisy who were brushing the dust that covered their clothes. Seizing the handle, he twisted it, trying to open the door but it was locked. He tugged at the handle again and again but it wouldn't budge.

"What now?" Kia asked.

"We need to distract them like Mr Peters said," Lewis explained.

"How?" Kia asked.

"I know what to do. Duck," Daisy shouted.

Daisy clutched a chair, hoping her plan wouldn't back fire on her as she tossed it at the plain glass door. Instantly the glass shattered, spreading pieces of glass across the floor as a loud crash echoed throughout the room, passing into the hallway.

Kia observed Daisy's moves, wondering why she did what she did without thinking of the consequences. They could hear moaning getting louder in the hallway as the zombies started moving slowly towards them. Within seconds the moaning stopped along with the zombie's footsteps as they swayed silently on the spot.

Lewis realised what she was doing as he noticed that the zombies had stopped moving because it was quiet again. They needed to get the zombies further away from the rest of their group. He joined Daisy as he picked up a chair and hurled it at the wall. One of the legs from the chairs broke off as it dropped to the ground, sending vibrations towards the zombies. Kia looked out of the door window as she saw the herd heading their way.

"It's working!" Kia shouted joyfully, "I can't see the others though. I can only see zombies and they're getting very close!"

Lewis and Daisy instantly stopped as a pair of zombie eyes peered through the broken glass door. Daisy grabbed Kia before the three of them ducked behind a desk trying to keep out of sight as they trembled with fear. They closed their eyes in hope to not see the zombies. They could hear a lot of movement and moaning from outside the room as the zombies scrambled to get inside.

Meanwhile Caitlyn, Josh, Kai, Scarlett and Mr Peters seized all the needles holding the cure which were in a bag as they quietly opened the door and entered the hallway. They could see the zombies had quickly moved towards another room which they could only guess had their friends in.

Josh suddenly jumped on a zombie, pushing it to the ground as Kai seized hold of its arms, pulling them behind the zombie's back. He carefully lifted it off the ground, not wanting to hurt it any more than he needed to as Mr Peters injected it with the cure. Caitlyn took the zombie from Kai as she put it into the room, shutting the door. She wanted to let it turn back to normal on its own.

They did it over and over again, seizing each one individually and passing it to the next person to do their job to help the process go quicker. They stuck to their four jobs; Josh seizing the zombies, Kai holding them while Mr Peters injected the cure into them and Caitlyn leading them into the room as she started walking around to each person who had changed, explaining what had happened to them.

Chapter 18
Never Safe

They heard loud clatters of furniture being thrown around coming from a room not too far away from them as they saw a few chairs fly into the hallway, missing a zombie by inches. Finally, they were on the last zombie. As they injected it, turning him back into a human, Mr Peters hastily ran to the room which had shattered glass outside of it as well as a few chairs.

Caitlyn followed him as she held a gun by her side for safety. They glanced at the broken door before barging their way into the room, being cautious of the shards of glass that stuck up from the door frame. Instantly Kia peered round from the desk, she scrambled to her feet as she ran straight to Caitlyn and gave her a massive hug of relief.

"I told you that you'd be okay," Caitlyn explained as they walked back to the room 179, holding hands.

When they arrived back, the room was filled with noisy chatter as everyone spoke to one and another in a confused and worried tone. Most of the people that they had cured where doctors, nurses or patients and even children that were in the building before it all had started. A few young children were chasing each other while their parents chatted.

They were all covered in blood and cuts which were slowly healing with the help of the cure. Everything seemed fine as some people laid down on the floor, bruised and exhausted whilst others leant against the wall trying to consider a scientific way for what had happened to them.

The room suddenly went into silence as a loud yell pierced its way through. There was a deafening silence as they all looked around, worriedly. It had come from outside. Everyone gazed out the window to see a pack of zombies corner a guy. They quickly shut their eyes as they heard a loud terrifying scream, remembering the once faded memories of how they become a zombie. The memory of how everything happened came clear as everyone fell back into the memory.

* A hospital in panic as more and more people with bite marks and scratches, covered in blood, screaming for help ran through the building. Many doctors stared at them in shock as one nurse reached out to help an injured man with six bullet holes in his body. Without hesitation the bloody man seized her by the neck and jammed his jaw into her flesh.

The nurse's scream echoed, she dropped to the floor as more flesh eaters arrived and pounced on her. Suddenly the lights turned off and they stood in utter darkness. Patients panicked as they squirmed in their beds, wanting to know what was happening. It didn't take long before nearly everyone in the hospital had been infected.

A few people escaped into the outside world, carrying the virus with them as they left the disease to overtake the hospital. Hoping to have left the gory trauma behind them, they ran home to their family's before turning into flesh eating monsters themselves and killing the ones they loved the most without knowing. *

"We need to get the cure out there!" Caitlyn explained, breaking the silence once again, bringing everyone back to reality.

"Don't you think I know that," Mr Peters answered, "but there's no way we can do that without dying!"

As soon as Mr Peters spoke, Daisy sprung her hand onto her head as a massive headache angrily thrashed against her skull. The room started spinning as her lips turned grey, along with the rest of her skin. Her legs felt like jelly as they gave up under the pressure of her body. She collapsed, letting Josh quickly catch her just before she touched the floor. Her eyes slowly started to shut as she tried her hardest to keep them open. Soon it was too much and her eyes closed.

"Daisy! Daisy! Please wake up! Daisy," Josh screamed.

Within a few minutes her eyes sprung open as josh saw they had turned pure red. She sprung towards Josh's neck with the look of hunger in her eyes. He tripped as he fell to the ground, trying to shove Daisy away from him, in fear of his life. She snapped her mouth, letting her teeth chatter together as she tried to bite him again.

Scarlett and Lewis tiptoed, trying to sneak up on her. She turned her head as they pounced on top of Daisy, pinning her to the floor as she snapped angrily at them. They held her arms flat on the ground, trying to stop both of their friends from dying.

Unfortunately for Lewis and Josh, Scarlett had begun turning back into a zombie as well. She dived towards Lewis, aiming for his arms. The same look that Daisy had was now spreading across Scarlett's face. Lewis tried his hardest to keep them both from biting him as everyone cowered away into the corners of the room.

"I don't understand how the cure didn't work," Mr Peters explained, "it should have worked!"

"If the cure didn't work, doesn't that mean the others will also change?" Caitlyn asked as she stood in front of Kia to protect her, "We're going to be surrounded by hundreds of zombies again!"

Caitlyn, Kia, Mr Peters, Kai, Josh and Lewis quickly turned around to see everyone on the floor shouting and twisting in agony as they began turning into vicious zombies. Caitlyn suddenly grasped hold of Kia as they ran out the door, taking her to another room for her own safety. She didn't want any harm to come to her, she was too young to have a fate as dreadful as turning into a flesh eating zombie.

"Stay here and don't move. I'll be back for you, I promise," Caitlyn said, giving her a hug before gently closing the door to the room that Kia was in.

Caitlyn ran back to the others but as she arrived, she saw Lewis and Josh pushing the zombie versions of Daisy and Scarlett off them. The five of them scuttled out of the room like cockroaches as they slammed the door shut behind without glancing back at the zombies that they were trapping inside.

Unfortunately, it didn't keep the zombies trapped for long. The zombies banged on the door, making it more unsteady with every knock. Gradually the door started creaking open as the weight of them broke it down. Slowly the zombies fell on top of each other, creating a large bundle of the deadly creatures. The five friends turned around as they saw the huddle lying in front of their feet.

Caitlyn screamed in shock as one of the zombies attacked her, seizing hold of her ankle. Its grip tightened as her skin turned red with pain. She fell to the ground, her ankle twisted as she screamed out in agony. Kai and Josh suddenly grabbed Caitlyn by the arms as they helped her to stand, pulling her swiftly out of the zombie's reach.

"Are you okay Cait?" Josh asked worriedly as he put her arm around his neck.

"I'll be fine, for now!" She replied.

"Good. I don't know what I'd do if anything had happened to you. You're my world!" Josh replied.

"About time you said it," Caitlyn answered as she leaned her face closer to his.

For a minute the world seemed to have stopped as if they were the only two people left on earth. Josh could feel his cheeks blushing as he leant in ready to kiss her. He had hoped for this moment for so long, when they would finally become one, letting nothing not even the apocalypse stand in their way.

Their lips slowly touched as they felt true happiness which neither of them had felt in a long time. Both of them knew what their lives now meant. They knew that they had to protect each other, no matter what as neither of them wanted to lose one another. A few loudly spoken words snapped them back into reality.

"Would you two stop kissing for one moment? We're still in danger if you hadn't realised," Lewis said.

"RUN!" Mr Peters shouted.

"You've doomed us all again!" Kai bellowed at Mr Peters.

"Do you want to stay and argue or run and maybe have a chance to live?" Mr Peters said sarcastically as he started running.

Kai looked around as he saw a crowd of zombies darting out of another door nearby. Lewis tumbled over a rotten copse, looking at it in disgust. He quickly turned around as a zombie got ready to pounce on him. Without a second thought, he seized his gun and begun shooting at the zombies as he was still laying on the ground.

Mr Peters grabbed hold of him, pulling him up as they left Kai, Josh and Caitlyn shooting the zombies. As soon as he had gained his strength to stand, he carried on shooting as he joined his friends wanting to help them. Not knowing whether they could cure the zombies now, they made every shot count as they aimed for the zombie's brains.

Kia could hear the gunshots being fired as she rushed out of the room that Caitlyn had put her in to keep her safe. Suddenly a zombie lunged at her neck. Ripping layer after layer of her flesh off, Kia screamed in agony, she squinted her eyes as tears flooded her reddened face. She shivered as her body went cold. Her pulse slowed down as more blood left her body.

Caitlyn gasped at the horrific sight of Kia bleeding out on the ground as she took out her knife, letting it pierce through the zombie's scalp. Blood oozed out as it dropped down dead on the floor in front of her feet.

"Kia, can you hear me?" Kai shouted as he darted towards her, pushing Caitlyn out of his way, "You can't die, not yet!"

More zombies were arriving on the scene. It seemed that they hadn't completely cleared the floor as they thought had been the case. Kai and Josh carefully lifted Kia into Caitlyn's arms. Kia's head fell backwards as her body went limp. The small group looked at the long corridor as they bolted for the doors to the stairs.

The zombies were a few feet behind them as they all hurried through the doors and down the stairs. Zombies bolted after them, trying to catch a delicious bite of their flesh as they carried on running for their lives. One zombie tripped as it stumbled down the stairs, inches away from all of them.

It fell beside Caitlyn and Kia, grabbing hold of Caitlyn's ankle and begun tugging at it to pull her over. Her leg gave in as she fell to the floor, her chin hitting the ground as blood trickled down. Everyone carried on running as Caitlyn tried to push Kia out of the zombie's reach but more had started to surround them.

"Leave me!" Kia chocked, spluttering blood on the steps below, "I'll turn soon, just go. Save yourself!"

"I can't just leave you Kia. You're like family to me," Caitlyn cried.

"I know it's hard to leave family behind, but your friends need you and my time is nearly up. Just find the cure and save the world!" Kia explained as her eyes began to shut.

Kia shoved Caitlyn as hard as she could with all her strength, letting her death seize hold. Josh and Lewis heard a loud scream as they saw Kia surrounded by zombies, feasting on her body. Caitlyn froze, wanting to run, but all her strength had left her body feeling hopeless as she sat on the steps crying.

Josh tugged at her sleeve, not wanting to leave Caitlyn alone with the horrific sight that would scar her for life. Knowing she wouldn't leave on her own, Kai grabbed one of her arms as Josh took the other, pulling her down the steps away from the scene. A loud yelp was heard as the rest of the team fled, reaching the bottom of the last flight of stairs.

They didn't want to stop and think about who had just died, knowing stopping for even one moment would make them all break down in tears. No one had time to feel sorry about their friend's deaths anymore because every second they wasted would be another precious moment they could spend fighting to survive.

"Get to the basement!" Mr Peters shouted, "It's the safest place in the entire building. I hope."

"No! You know what, I've had enough. Kia just died because of you," Caitlyn said, beginning to cry.

"Caitlyn… I know how much you cared for her, I loved her too more than any of you will ever know but we can't start blaming people. We need to carry on moving, otherwise we'll be dead too," Kai explained, trying to comfort Caitlyn.

Caitlyn sprinted off in tears, not wanting to hear another word from anyone as Josh ran after her. Mr Peters stood next to Kai and Lewis awkwardly as they ignored each other. No one wanted to speak after what had just happened. Lewis could feel his throat going dry as he tried not to cry himself. He had lost three people today; two of his closest friends and one person he had only known for a short while but it had felt a lot longer.

Kai had promised his mother that he would look after little Kia, that he wouldn't let any harm come to her but now Kia was gone and there was nothing he could do to change it. He hated this new reality that all of them were trapped in now. Every day they were losing more of their loved ones as they tried to save the planet from complete destruction.

Chapter 19
A Cure for a Bullet

"They're coming! Get to that cupboard now!" Mr Peters shouted as he heard zombies moaning, swiftly making their way down the stairs.

"What about Caitlyn and Josh?" Kai replied.

"They'll have to find a hiding place if they want to live!" Mr Peters replied.

Lewis scurried to the door, throwing it wide open as the three of them darted inside. They stood in utter darkness as Mr Peters felt his way around the wall, searching for a light switch. Eventually he found it as he flicked it on. Once again they stood in silence staring at the cupboard which they were in.

The cupboard seemed a lot bigger, more like a small room cluttered with paper work. There were shelves full of old books covered in dust with splatters of blood on top. A bloody trail dripped down the wall from the ceiling vent above.

A blood covered gun lay in the corner of room, shinning as the light flickered on it. A light grey paint concealed the walls as ripped posters hung loosely off them. Splatters of blood stood out on the wooden floor as the three of them watched their steps.

Lewis broke the deadly silence which felt as if it was burning away at their souls. He opened the door to the cupboard a little, letting a loud creaking sound echo through the room. A gruesome zombie's hand suddenly grabbed hold of him as it tried to pull him out of the room.

The zombie had short brown hair covered in blood. It had flesh hanging loosely from the neck bone with part of its left eyebrow missing with a large slice cut in it. The creature's hair was stuck to its bloody face like glue as it peeped its head through the door. Lewis screamed as he tried to pull himself away. Neither Kai nor Mr Peters had even noticed as they were too busy arguing with each other.

"IT'S ENTIRELY YOUR FAULT!" Kai screamed at Mr Peters.

"Help me," Lewis shouted, kicking the zombie in its distorted head as he was ignored.

"She was your responsibility; I wasn't the one who brought her here. You did, all of you or did you forget?" Mr Peters answered.

"It's not my fault, your stupid cure didn't work!" Kai shouted.

"At least I'm trying to end the apocalypse. I've tried to save humanity. I've tried to create a cure. What have you done? Except for running around like a headless chicken!" Mr Peters replied.

"I brought all of us here to help save the world, that's what I have done!"

"You tried to help, don't make me laugh. You made it worse, you brought the virus with you. You made a scene so the halls got flooded with zombies. You helped kill your friends!"

"Shut the hell up, both of you and help me!" Lewis screamed.

It seemed that it didn't matter how much Lewis screamed for help, they were too busy shouting at each other to notice him. Without warning, Josh suddenly fell from the ceiling vent as he crashed to the floor, separating Kai and Mr Peters. Josh looked up as he noticed the zombie fighting Lewis.

He stood up and ran to him. Even though he hardly knew Lewis, he didn't want to lose any one else today as he had already lost his sister to the blood thirsty virus. He started pulling Lewis away as he gripped hold of him by his arm. At last Kai and Mr Peters noticed what was happening to them.

They both stopped shouting as they quickly rushed over to offer their help but as they did they realised who the zombie was. Its brown hair flicked back out of its face, showing who the zombie once was. It was Daisy, Josh's beloved sister. He stopped as he stared at his blood covered zombie sister. The sight finally made Josh stop and think about the reality they were really facing.

He was speechless, he didn't think that he would ever see his sister again especially after she had turned into the monster that she had become. It was a horrific sight, seeing more zombies clamber on top of her as they tried to climb over in order to get them.

"I can't believe what she's turned into," Josh said quietly staring at the door.

"It is part of life now," Mr Peters answered as he grabbed hold of Lewis.

He pulled him away from the door to save his life. Kai slammed the door shut as soon as Lewis was out of the way. All of a sudden Caitlyn returned to the group as she burst through the ceiling. As she landed on the floor, she heard her elbow crack as she gripped hold of it in pain.

"It wouldn't be a part of life, if it wasn't thanks to you and your stupid experiment," Josh replied angrily.

"I was only following orders," Mr Peters said, "It was my job. They wouldn't let me say no."

Caitlyn stood next to Josh; she took hold of his hands as she leant in to rest her head on his shoulder. A tear rolled down her face at the thought of her friends becoming flesh eating monsters. She couldn't believe how many people she had lost in a small amount of time; it didn't feel real, none of it did. It felt like a nightmare which never seemed to end.

"Who gave you the orders?" Caitlyn asked, breaking her from her thoughts.

"That's classified information," Mr Peters said.

"You've killed hundreds of innocent people because of that virus," Caitlyn started speaking, "You really think I care if it's classified or not! Now tell me before I do something that I'll regret!"

Everyone could hear the moaning and growling coming from the stairs as they guessed more zombies had arrived to block them in. A loud smash could be heard from the other side of the door as they screamed out in terror. Josh seized hold of Caitlyn, wrapping her into a tight comforting hug as he never wanted to let her go.

"If this is the end, I want you to spend it in my arms," Josh explained.

Caitlyn looked at him and smiled as she snuggled her head further into his neck. Once again they heard a loud thud smash the door as a hand made its way through. Lewis jumped backwards, almost falling into Kai and Mr Peters. They backed away from the door, not wanting to be anywhere near it just in case.

The cupboard door suddenly burst off its hinges as all the zombies stumbled in. Caitlyn, Josh, Mr Peters, Kai and Lewis froze to the spot as all the zombies surrounded them, blocking the exit. They could feel their bodies trembling in fear as the zombies got closer. Tears flooded out of Lewis's and Caitlyn's eyes as Lewis hid his face from his friends. Josh tried to stay strong for Caitlyn as he held his feelings back.

The zombies looked hungrier than ever as they stumbled closer and closer, dying for a bite of their flesh. Three zombies stood out against the rest; one with short brown hair which they already knew was Daisy. There was another with long brown hair tied up in a ponytail; blood covered the freckles on its face which made them think it was Kia. The last zombie that stood out against the rest they could tell was Scarlett due to her different shades of blue hair.

They were just like the rest of the zombies, trying to dive at their friends for a feast. What were they supposed to do? There was nothing that they could do, or was there? They felt like mice caught in a trap, they were stuck and there was nothing they could do about it.

"We're going to die!" Lewis said.

"Would you stop being so negative? Even for one small minute" Kai replied.

"Oh so I'm supposed to be all positive when we're about to die then," Lewis said sarcastically, "Well sorry if I don't feel happy about dying!"

They were trapped. Feeling hopeless and alone, everyone cowered tightly together in a small group. Caitlyn suddenly noticed something odd about one of the zombies which was getting closer to them. Its eyes were flickering between red and a normal light green. She looked at it confused. What did it mean? She elbowed Josh as she pointed at the creature.

"Mr Peters look!" Josh whispered pointing to the zombies flickering eyes, "Maybe the cure is working after all!"

The zombie with the flickering eyes suddenly dropped to the floor. They stared at it in shock, not knowing what to do as they stayed in a huddle. It gasped for air as it shivered on the cold hard ground. Lewis took a few steps forward, slowly approaching it but as he did, it grabbed him by the scruff of his shirt making him scream in shock.

The zombie looked him in his eyes as if he could see a real person and not just another walking meal. Lewis felt a part of his soul move towards the zombie as its hands dropped to the floor, not moving.

"What's happening?" Kai said as he looked at the other zombies which surrounded them.

The zombies stopped dead in their tracks, frozen like statues as they looked straight ahead of them. Their eyes started to flicker just like the first zombie's eyes did as they dropped to the floor. They screamed in agony as they twisted their bodies painfully. Was the cure working? Was the zombie apocalypse finally about to come to an end?

"It looks like their zombie forms are fighting with their human forms. We might actually get to live, hopefully," Mr Peters explained, "That must be one of the side effects."

"Well if that's true, then we might not turn into zombies after all!" Caitlyn said, "That would mean we've saved the world!"

"Maybe this cure of yours won't kill us after all," Kai replied, "If we live, then I apologise for everything I said."

"So do I," Mr Peters replied, "I'm sorry for being so rude."

"It's fine, I guess I was asking for it. I could have been politer," Lewis answered.

Every zombie in the room was now on the floor, rolling and turning in agony. Their eyes were twitching as they flickered from red to a natural colour. They all fought against themselves as they tried to return back to normal. A few of them were strong enough to instantly return to normal as Scarlett ran over in tears and hugged Kai. As soon as her arms wrapped around him, her stomach filled with butterfly's that were flying out of control. She couldn't love him as she knew he loved Kia and Kia loved him.

"I knew you would be okay. You're a fighter," Kai explained.

"I'll always be a fighter as long as I have something worth fighting for," Scarlett replied, smiling at him.

Scarlett couldn't hide her feelings forever as much as she hated to admit it. She quickly pushed him away carefully as she stopped hugging him. He looked at her with a confused expression before noticing a lot more people had started turning back to their original selves. Everyone was stronger than they had thought they would be.

Mr Peters looked at everyone; knowing that everything that had happened was his fault, including his daughter's death. Loads of people had died in the last few weeks, so many good hearted people who didn't deserve such a tragic ending.

"Thank you," Scarlett said to Mr Peters for the first time ever without sarcasm, meaning every word.

Finally, all the zombies had been taken over by their true forms once again, turning them back into humans. Their eyes had turned back to their original colour just like the rest of their bodies. They weren't evil flesh eating zombies anymore, they were normal human beings.

Josh looked into the crowd of people lying on the floor and spotted Daisy who was coughing badly. She opened her eyes to see Josh kneeling beside her with tears pouring out of his eyes. They smiled happily as they wrapped their arms around each other. Daisy's eyes felt heavy with exhaustion as she tried her hardest to keep them open.

"Daisy you're okay!" Josh said joyfully.

"Of course I am," Daisy replied.

Josh stood up as he held his hand out for Daisy, wanting to help her off the floor. She took hold of his hand as she struggled to gain strength to stand up. After a few minutes of standing still, staring at each other, they thought of what to do next as Kia got up off the floor and limped towards her group.

Kia collapsed to the floor in pain as Caitlyn ran over to her. Caitlyn reached for Kia as she gave her a reassuring hug, wanting to comfort her. Kia yawned, covering her mouth. Even though she felt exhausted from what had happened, she still wanted to be polite and cover her mouth when she was yawning.

"Are you okay?" Caitlyn said looking at Kia nervously.

"I'm just tired," Kia replied, "I'll be fine."

"BINGO! The cure can be transmitted by blood too", Mr Peters yelled happily as he realised Kia hadn't had the cure injected into her like the others.

Chapter 20
Spirits of the Past

"Are you sure you're not hurt?" Caitlyn asked worriedly.
"I'm a bit sore but apart from that I'm fine," Kia replied.
Kia carried on hugging Caitlyn as they both started crying with joy. Neither of them had thought they would ever see each other again but they were both proven wrong. Caitlyn knew that Kia had no living family that she knew of and felt bad. What was Kia going to do when the apocalypse ended? Who would she live with? Caitlyn knew that she was old enough to take care of her but she didn't know if Kia wanted that.

"I have something to ask you," Caitlyn started talking, "I know your parents aren't alive and I know your sister might be but until we know for sure, would you like to come and live with me?"

"Of course, I would love to but we have to find my sister too," Kia said, "We won't stop searching for her, will we?"

"Of course we won't! We'll carry on searching for her till we reach the end of the earth," Caitlyn replied.

"Thank you."

While they had been busy talking, loads of people had got up off the floor and ran towards their loved ones. Suddenly everyone's eye fell upon Mr Peters, they heard zombies arriving at the front door to the building as they began hitting the windows viciously. It would take them longer than they had thought to cure everyone. Due to not having enough, they needed to make more.

"Lewis and Kai follow me. We need to make more," Mr Peters said as he opened the door to the room that they were in and headed for the stairs, "Everyone else keep the zombies out."

"And don't argue!" Daisy shouted, "You need to focus on the task."

Lewis and Kai looked at each other, giving a small chuckle before hastily running up the stairs after Mr Peters. Daisy, Josh, Caitlyn, Scarlett and Kia stood still staring at each other as they chatted away happily. All of a sudden one of the windows by the main door smashed, making everyone's heads quickly turn around as they closed the door to the cupboard a little.

It felt like a long time but only a few minutes had passed. Lewis and Kai ran down the stairs with boxes of injections, each full with the serum. Every person who was in the cupboard rushed to the front doors trying to keep the zombies out as Daisy and Scarlett sneaked over to Lewis and Kai.

"Everyone grab some injections and hide. Scarlett and I are going to open the doors. Once the doors are open and you see a zombie you have to inject them and put them in a room," Kai explained.

"Okay," everyone replied in unison as they grabbed some injections.

People darted off in all directions with the injections as they started to hide. Some hid in the closest rooms that they could find while some hid behind walls. Kai took Scarlett by the hand as he lent in for a kiss. Scarlett closed her eyes as their lips touched. For a few minutes the real world disappeared as if it was just the two of them.

"What about Kia?" Scarlett asked.

"What about her?" Kai replied.

"Don't you love her?" Scarlett asked.

"Of course I love her but not in the same way as I love you!" He said.

The two of them paced over to the doors as they opened them, letting the zombies fly in. Scarlett and Kai started running for their lives, as more zombies appeared.

"If we die, I want you to know that you're the most amazing girl I've ever known and I'm glad that we met," Kai explained as they ran holding hands.

"If we do die, I want you to know that you're the sweetest guy and I'm glad you found us that night," Scarlett said as she gave him a little smirk.

"I love you," they both said to each other as they began running with their hands tightly sealed together.

Zombies ran after them as loads of people jumped out, jabbing the zombies with the cure before dragging them into different rooms and leaving them alone to change and fight for their human side. They knew that it would be dangerous if they were in the same room as the people that were changing. It would be a danger to them all.

Two zombies pounced onto Scarlett and Kai, pushing them to the ground as they tried to feast upon them. Luckily for them a young man with a Mohawk arrived just in time. He wore an open shirt which showed his thin body with a pair of blue skinny trousers. On his back he had a rucksack which was over filled with injections.

The young man jumped onto the zombie's back, throwing them off Scarlett and Kai as he pinned one to the floor, letting Kai pin the other. He grabbed an injection and handed it over to Kai as he took out another. The two boys injected the cure into the zombie's backs.

"Thank you," Scarlett and Kai said to the young man.

"Don't mention it," the young man replied before running after other zombies with the cure held out in front of him.

It took a few hours to trap all the zombies inside different rooms, allowing them to change back into their human forms. After the first change, they turned back into zombies before fighting to turn back into humans once again.

"I can't believe that it will be over soon," Caitlyn said.

"None of us will be the same though," Josh explained, "Not after everything that's happened."

Even though everyone knew that the apocalypse was a bad thing, it had destroyed so many lives but in the same way it was good; it brought everyone closer together, people that hadn't known each other and wouldn't have if it wasn't due to the virus escaping. Everyone in the world did their part to save the human race from extinction.

Many people were running around injecting the serum into those that had been infected outside the hospital. They had all found where they belonged, after all everyone has a place in this world. It doesn't matter how big or small it is, all that matters is that you know you're important and someday even you could help save the world.

A few days after the cure had finally been spread; Daisy and her friends were walking through the streets helping to clean up the mess that had been left behind. To their surprise they found Ella's body lying on the streets in the same place as they last saw her. She faded into the rubbish as if she was a piece herself, left to get thrown away. They were all shocked and saddened to see her like this as there wasn't much remaining of her.

They knew even if they gave her the cure, she would be in so much pain and would die immediately. It wouldn't be right to bring her back just to watch her die all over again. Daisy couldn't bring herself to do that to one of her best friends as they covered her body up with a blanket.

Daisy made sure Ella had a proper funeral which her closest friends and family could attend to say their final goodbyes. Through everything they had lost, they still had their humanity left and that was important in a zombified world. Days passed quickly after the zombie apocalypse had nearly destroyed the world along with the human race and everything on the planet.

The world became a better place after all of the horror and tragedy had finally come to an end. Many lives were lost to the apocalypse including Ella, Zack, Amy and Adam but slowly the survivors were learning to deal with their loss and everything that had happened. They knew that they were stronger; physically and mentally for everything that they had faced.

Many leaders had either left or died when the world went to hell, so there was no one left to lead the remaining survivors. Josh had looked after everyone within the group as if they were one big family, not caring about who they once were before it all happened. They had all decided to leave their past where it belonged, safely hidden where no one could judge them again.

No-one else was ready to lead what was left of the population, except from Josh who knew he could help save more lives by rebuilding the population to make a safer world for all of them to live in, one that wasn't going to be destroyed by greed and hatred.

As Zack's funeral day got closer, Daisy got more emotional as she cried out for him. Finally, the day arrived and it was time to say goodbye forever. Tears ran down her face as something frozen almost ice like touched her cheeks, sending a shiver through her body, wiping her tears away.

A beautiful white shadow of Zack hovered in front. He smiled as he was gently floated towards her, wearing a white suit and gold chains dangling loosely around his neck. On his right hand he had two gold rings one engraved with his name and the other engraved with her name.

On his suit he had one red rose pinned to his left pocket with a piece of paper popping out as he took hold of it, placing it firmly into his bony hands. He reached out his hand to hold hers but his hand slipped straight through, he tried again and again until the paper in his hand vanished.

Zack's shadow smiled as he started fading away, disappearing into a white fog. Another tear ran down her face but this time it was a tear of happiness as she watched him leave for the very last time. He was gone now. He could finally rest in peace.

"I'll always remember you Zacky," Daisy whispered.

"I'll always love you Dais," Zack replied as his voice faded away with him.

She felt something cold in her hand making her shiver as she looked down, she saw an old photo bent in half with her and Zack from their childhood with one of his gold rings sellotaped to it. His name glowed as she unstuck it from the photo before putting the ring on. Daisy held the photo close to her heart as she let Zack's body rest for the last time.

She remembered something Josh said when they were younger, "just because you can't see them, doesn't mean they're not with you."

"Are you okay sis?" Josh asked as he sat next to Daisy.

"I will be. Just because I can't see him doesn't mean he's not here," she replied.

"That's the spirit," Caitlyn said as she walked over to them.

Everyone felt much better after the funeral had ended. They all had their chances to say goodbye to their loved ones for the last time as they could finally move on with their lives. The roads were clear; cars were parked neatly on the yellow lines.

Most of the buildings looked brand new as they stood tall, towering high over the town. Caitlyn, Josh, Daisy and Kia walked through the town, talking happily to each other as a person darted towards them on their hands and feet. Kia screamed as Daisy pulled her out of the way.

The creature stared at them with its bright red eyes bulging out of its skin as they ducked behind a dumpster. It sniffed the air as it slowly walked towards them before grabbing hold of the dumpster and throwing it away, letting trash soar through the air, scattering the roads with rubbish as they screamed in shock.

They ran; too frightened to look back at the horrifying creature. The beast had razor sharp bloody teeth that were covered with blackish green mould as it drooled showing a green slime that dangled from its grey crackled lips. Its black fingernails were long and sharp, ready to rip something or someone apart.

Slowly it ran after them, gathering up speed as it kept its eyes on its prey. Daisy suddenly screamed as it hurtled towards her as it threw its body in front of her. It growled as it slashed its massive palms at her. Skipping backwards, she dodged its slash of anger as it once again went for her.

Its claws were out stretched as it sliced across her face before pushing her down. She collapsed as her head slammed against the solid ground. Covered in slices from the creature's claws, she laid lifeless. Blood oozing out of her head as the beast threw her over its shoulders before darting off into the night, leaving only Daisy's jumper behind.

Caitlyn grabbed her jumper as the three of them rushed after the dangerous beast, not wanting to lose Daisy to the creature that was terrorising everyone. They didn't know what had caused this human to change but they did know that they weren't going to lose Daisy after everything they had been through.

They were a family now and a family always has each other's back. The three of them carried on running after the creature as they saw a door swing open, swallowing the shadow of Daisy and the beast within. They stood by the door, not knowing what to expect as the door creaked open. A pair of glowing red eyes stared back at them before vanishing into the darkness, leaving Daisy unconscious in the hallway.

Her friends rushed over to her, not knowing what to do next as fear flooded through their bodies, making them tremble at the thought of what might happen next. What was that creature? Was there a new virus? Would they survive?

The End Or Is It?

CPSIA information can be obtained
at www.ICGtesting.com
Printed in the USA
LVHW022147170221
679360LV00007B/460